"You'd better call Sheriff Armstrong. Somebody's slouched over in the front seat of my
truck."

. . . said Mor Pendleton.

Alex felt a chill grip his heart. "Passed out or dead?"

"Dead," Mor said simply, and Emma started sobbing
softly beside him, collapsing against Mor for support. It
had to be a shock, finding a body in the cab of the truck
like that.

As Mor reached for the telephone, Alex asked, "Any
idea who it was?"

Mor nodded, looking grim as he dialed the sheriff's
number. "I'd never seen him before in my life, but Emma
recognized him right away. Hang on a second, I only want
to have to say this once." Mor turned his attention back to
the telephone. "Sheriff, this is Mor Pendleton. You'd better get to Hatteras West. Somebody just killed Emma Sturbridge's ex-husband."

A LIGHTHOUSE INN MYSTERY

"Book me at Hatteras West any day!"
—Tamar Myers, author of *Gruel and Unusual Punishment*

Lighthouse Inn Mysteries by Tim Myers

INNKEEPING WITH MURDER
RESERVATIONS FOR MURDER
MURDER CHECKS INN
ROOM FOR MURDER

ROOM FOR MURDER

Tim Myers

BERKLEY PRIME CRIME, NEW YORK

ROOM FOR MURDER

A Berkley Prime Crime Book / published by arrangement with the author

PRINTING HISTORY
Berkley Prime Crime mass-market edition / September 2003

ISBN: 0-425-19310-1

Berkley Prime Crime Books are published by The Berkley Publishing Group, a division of Penguin Group (USA) Inc., 375 Hudson Street, New York, New York 10014. The name BERKLEY PRIME CRIME and the BERKLEY PRIME CRIME design are trademarks belonging to Penguin Group (USA) Inc.

PRINTED IN THE UNITED STATES OF AMERICA

10   9   8   7   6   5   4   3   2   1

For Patty and Emily,
My Reasons Why.

1

"I can't believe you're actually letting these blowhards take over the Grand Unveiling like this," Mor Pendleton said as he and Alex Winston watched the activities on the temporary outdoor stage from the wings of the newly rebuilt Dual Keepers' Quarters of the Hatteras West Inn. A long shadow fell from the nearby lighthouse, hiding them from the view of most of the crowd. Mor was not only the town handyman who helped keep Hatteras West in good repair, he also happened to be Alex's best friend in the world.

Alex said, "What can I say, I'm shameless. I can use every bit of free publicity I can get for the inn, and I figured having both mayoral candidates come out for the festivities might get us some good press." Alex owned and operated the Hatteras West Inn, a hostelry featuring a duplicate of the Cape Hatteras Lighthouse and Keepers' Quarters tucked away in the foothills of the Blue Ridge Mountains.

Things were definitely looking up, Alex thought, as he surveyed the new construction. With the completion of the building, Hatteras West finally felt whole again; the absence of the main building had been like a missing tooth for the lighthouse and the smaller Main Keeper's Quarters. Better yet, maybe now they could actually operate at a profit again.

Elise Danton, the Hatteras West Inn's housekeeper who was indispensable in running the place, came up behind them and said, "Mor, Emma's been looking all over for you. She says it's important."

The big man shrugged. "She must not be looking that hard. I've been right here all afternoon." Emma Sturbridge and Mor Pendleton had survived more than a few rough patches in their rocky relationship, and Alex often wondered where the two would finally end up when the smoke cleared.

Elise smiled softly. "I'll just go tell her where to find you then."

Mor said abruptly, "No need for that. I'll track her down myself. I've got a pretty good idea about what's on her mind." There was something about the big man's smile that made Alex pause. Something was definitely in the air today.

After Mor was gone, Elise moved up beside Alex and said, "This is so wonderful. We've finally got the inn back the way it should be."

Alex said, "Just in time, too. We used up the last of the money from the emerald sale, but it was worth it, wasn't it? It turned out better than I'd even hoped." One of Alex's guests at the inn had discovered a vein of emeralds somewhere on the Winston property, only to take the secret of its location to the grave with her. However, there had been enough quality emeralds found in her possession to pay for rebuilding the Dual Keepers' Quarters, finally restoring the property to its original splendor.

The audience suddenly broke loose with applause. It took Alex a second to realize they were clapping for Tracy Shook, one of the two candidates vying for Grady Hatch's job as mayor of Elkton Falls. Tracy, a petite blonde around Alex's age, was nearly hidden by the podium onstage. Alex had grown up with Tracy and her ex-husband, Conner Shook. Though Tracy and Conner had shared the same last name throughout their lives, the two came from opposite branches of the Shook family tree, so far separated that they were less blood-kin than many of the folks who lived in Elkton Falls. Tracy, now running for mayor, had hyphenated her line of Shooks onto her married name, but she'd dropped her husband's Shook the day their divorce was finalized. In Alex's opinion, Tracy was what Elkton Falls government needed: someone with fresh ideas and a new approach to shake things up. Conner, predictably enough, was acting as her competitor's campaign manager.

As Tracy's opponent, Oxford Hitchcock, took the stage for his own speech, Alex asked, "Elise, is everything ready inside?"

They were having a reception in the lobby of the new building after the speeches were finished, and he wanted to make sure everything was just right.

"The punch is chilling, the finger foods are on their trays, and I've got three college kids decked out in their finest to serve our guests. I heard the chamber group warming up a few minutes ago, and they sounded wonderful."

Alex said, "I'm still not sure about classical music at Hatteras West. It's a little highbrow for Elkton Falls, don't you think?"

She patted his arm. "Alex, don't worry, everyone will love it."

"I still say we should have gone with a bluegrass band."

Elise said, "The next time we have a building dedication, we'll do just that."

Alex sighed. "To be honest with you, I never want to have to go through this again."

"That makes two of us. But don't worry so much, our troubles are over."

On the stage, Oxford was wrapping up his comments, praising apple pie and motherhood, and the crowd roared again. Oxford was a popular man around Elkton Falls, serving on the Town Council for twelve years as well as handling the treasurer's duties. He was a stout, heavyset man with a full mane of silver hair and a voice that echoed through the hills. As he spoke, Oxford locked both thumbs under his "signature" suspenders.

Oxford Hitchcock was in sharp contrast to Tracy Shook in just about every way: he bellowed, while she always spoke softly, and though Oxford could put away more food than any man, woman, or child at one of his political barbeque events, Tracy never seemed to do more than nibble around the edges of her plate. Oxford was massive and barrel-chested, while she was a slender woman with the biggest blue eyes Alex had ever seen.

Tracy and Alex had been friends since elementary school and had stayed close. Tracy and her ex-husband Conner, on the other hand, had grown to dislike each other more and more over the years following their divorce. Conner was running Oxford's mayoral campaign, and the general consensus at Buck's Grill was that the only reason he worked with such enthusiasm was to rob Tracy of her chance for victory.

Longtime Mayor Grady Hatch took the stage as Oxford walked off, and for the first time that day, the applause was across the board, genuine and heartfelt. Grady had been running Elkton Falls since Alex had been a kid. The mayor's face was flushed, and there was a rasp in his voice as he talked to the crowd. "Well now, I'm sure you'all are tired of the sound of my voice after all these years, so I'll make this brief." There was a burst of laughter from the audience, since Grady was notorious for his clipped comments in public.

"Even more so than usual," Grady added with a smile. He was clearly enjoying his last days in office, with most of the petty squabbles of his political life left behind. Grady had stunned Elkton Falls when he'd announced that he wouldn't be seeking reelection. Folks were just starting to realize they'd been taking him for granted all along, but no one could talk him into changing his mind. For weeks, Grady had told anyone who would listen that the second he left office, he was going to buy a motor home and see the world. The only thing Grady had promised to participate in after leaving office was the "Save the Bridge" fund, a committee Alex had grudgingly agreed to serve on himself, since he believed so strongly in its cause. Elkton Falls sported one of the last covered bridges still standing in North Carolina, and Grady had made it his personal cause in life to see the bridge restored with private money when Raleigh had turned down his request for preservation funding.

Grady told the crowd, "Save your applause for someone who really deserves it. We're here to celebrate the dedication of this fine structure," he said, gesturing to the new building, "and the man who made it happen. Alex, come on up here and say a few words."

Alex shook his head numbly. He absolutely hated speaking in public.

Elise gave him a nudge. "Go on, Alex."

"I can't," he said. Why had Grady done this to him? Alex would rather take a beating than talk in front of all those people.

She nudged him and said, "You can do it, Alex. Don't look at the crowd.

"Focus on me," she added as the applause started to fade.

Alex took in a deep gulp of air and walked toward the stage like a man on his way to his doom.

As he approached the microphone, he walked past the mayor and whispered, "Grady, I'll get you for this."

The mayor chuckled. "You'll have to stand in line, my boy. There are a lot of folks with bigger grudges than yours waiting to take a shot at me."

Alex walked up to the microphone as panic swept through him. Everyone was staring at him! He fought the urge to bolt from the platform as his frantic gaze found Elise. Taking a deliberately deep breath, Alex kept his gaze on her as he said, "Thanks for coming, everybody. Now let's all go inside and enjoy the refreshments and music."

It was by far the shortest speech of the day, and the crowd showed their appreciation with enthusiastic applause. As they filed past the stage to tour the newly completed building, Grady grabbed Alex's shoulder.

"Your speech was even shorter than mine," the mayor said. "I'll make a public speaker out of you yet."

Alex said, "That's going to be tough to do, Grady. You just witnessed my debut and farewell performance, all wrapped up into one."

Grady shook his head. "We'll just see about that. Folks around here have a real fondness for you, Alex; you could do well in politics."

Alex shook his head in reply. "No Sir, it's not going to happen." He looked all around for Elise, and Alex finally spotted her greeting folks on their way into the newly rebuilt Dual Keepers' Quarters. That was where he belonged, by her side, instead of up there making speeches, however brief. Alex was an innkeeper, like his father before him, and his father before him, and he was proud to be one. Let the politicians have the limelight; they were welcome to it. The only light he wanted was the one he had, perched atop the lighthouse.

As Alex started off the stage, Tracy stopped him. "Alex, thanks again for letting me speak here today. I need all the exposure I can get."

He smiled. "You're very welcome. How's the campaign going?"

She looked a little frazzled around the edges. "I'm definitely the underdog, so it's a lot harder than I thought it would be. *He's* making it even worse." Tracy added the last jab as she stared heatedly at her ex-husband, standing off to one side in a whispered conference with Oxford.

Alex said, "Don't look at it that way, Tracy. Just think how sweet it will be when you beat him."

"Do you really think I've got a chance?" she asked.

"Hey, I'm voting for you," Alex said.

Just then Oxford's booming voice sounded in his ear. "I hope you give me the opportunity to change your mind, Alex."

Alex grinned. "You can try, but I won't make any promises."

Oxford returned the smile. "Then you wouldn't go far in politics, my friend." The big man turned his attention to Tracy, automatically tucking his thumbs back under his suspenders. "That was a wonderful speech, Ma'am. I had to stop myself from jumping up and applauding myself."

She said sweetly, "If you want to concede now, Oxford, we can save Elkton Falls the trouble of holding the election."

Oxford's smile dimmed a bit, though he could clearly see that Tracy was teasing. He said, "Come now, what fun would that be? I think we're all looking forward to the battle ahead. Now if you two will excuse me, I've got some meeting and greeting to do."

Tracy followed closely on his heels. "Not without me, you don't."

Alex was surprised to find Mor and Emma standing so close to the chamber group when he got inside. They were obviously hovering there for some reason. He walked over to Elise, pointed to their friends, and asked, "What's going on?"

"It's a surprise. I told them they could make a little announcement of their own today. I hope that's all right, Alex."

"You run this place, too, Elise. You can do whatever you like." Alex was a little hurt that Mor hadn't asked him for permission himself, and Elise must have sensed it.

She explained, "Emma's been planning this for a week. Mor just found out himself."

"So what's going on?"

The musicians stopped, and Elise whispered, "Wait and see."

As the group took a break, Mor said loudly, "If I can have your attention, there's something I'd like to say."

Everyone stopped talking and turned to the big man. Alex could see the flush rising on his friend's face. He was no more comfortable talking in front of a crowd than Alex was.

Once Mor had everyone's attention, he said, "Emma and I wanted to share this with everyone. We're getting married." There was more robust applause for Mor's announcement than there'd been for any of the politicians earlier. Mor added, "As a matter of fact, the nuptials will be here, if Alex will have us."

Alex smiled broadly from across the room. "Try to have your wedding anywhere else. Just tell me when."

"One month from today, and everyone's invited to the party," Mor said as the crowd roared again. As people filed past them offering their congratulations, Alex tapped Elise on the shoulder. He asked, "So you've known about this for a week?"

Elise grinned. "Are you kidding? I'm the maid of honor."

Alex said, "I don't even know which side of the aisle I'm supposed to sit on."

Elise started to say something when Mor joined them. "Alex, got a second?"

"Sure thing. Congratulations." He slapped the big man on the back.

"Thanks. Listen, sorry to spring it on you like that, but Emma and Elise cooked this all up. You don't mind having the wedding here, do you?"

"I couldn't think of a better place for you to have it," Alex said. "I'm honored."

"That's great. While I'm on a roll, let me push my luck a little more, then. How about being my best man?"

Alex grinned. "I'd be happy to." A cloud crossed his face as he added softly, "Oh, no."

"What's wrong?" Mor asked. "You don't have to do it if you don't want to."

"It's not that, I'm honored you want me. I just realized I'll have to make another speech if I'm going to be your best man."

Mor pounded him gamely on the shoulder. "You'll do fine. Look at all the practice you've been getting lately."

•   •   •

After the reception was over, Mor and Emma were the last ones to leave. Alex marveled that his two good friends had actually decided to get married. Here he was, waiting for his first promised date with Elise, and Mor and Emma were already tying the knot. His much-anticipated first date with his housekeeper wasn't far away, though; it was set for that coming Saturday night. Alex and Elise were free of their encumbrances and entanglements, so finally they were going to be able to see if there was anything more to their relationship than just friendship.

After the betrothed pair left, Alex and Elise began to clean up the mess left behind.

"The wedding's going to be beautiful," Elise said as she finished sweeping the lobby floor.

Alex said, "It looks like I'll be a part of it after all. Mor just asked me to be his best man."

Elise's budding smile froze as Mor and Emma walked back into the lobby. It was obvious from one look at their faces that something was desperately wrong.

"What happened?" Alex asked, afraid that the engagement was already off.

Mor said, "You'd better call Sheriff Armstrong. Somebody's slouched over in the front seat of my truck."

Alex felt an icy fist clench his heart. "Passed out or dead?"

"Dead," Mor said simply, and Emma started sobbing softly beside him, collapsing against Mor for support.

As Mor reached for the telephone, Alex asked, "Any idea who it is?"

Mor nodded, looking grim as he dialed the sheriff's number. "I'd never seen him before in my life, but Emma recognized him right away. Hang on a second, I only want to have to say this once." Mor turned his attention back to the telephone. "Sheriff, this is Mor Pendleton. You'd better get out to Hatteras West. I just found a body in my truck."

There was a pause, then Mor added grimly, "Yes, we know who it is. Somebody just killed Emma Sturbridge's ex-husband."

2

After Mor hung up the telephone, Alex said, "This is incredible. Any idea what happened?"

Mor snapped, "What makes you think I would know? I've heard enough horror stories about the man to want to beat the daylights out of him myself, but I wouldn't kill him. He was a brute and a bully, Alex, but I swear, I never saw him before today in my life."

Elise guided Emma over to one side of the lobby, one arm around the woman's shoulders. The two of them talked in whispered murmurs.

Alex asked Mor softly, "What did Emma have to say?"

Mor said, "She was just as stunned as I was. What was he doing here, Alex? And how did he end up in my truck? This looks bad, I know that, but I swear, somebody's trying to set me up."

Alex said, "Don't worry, Sheriff Armstrong will be here soon."

Mor snorted. "And that's supposed to make me feel better? Alex, how would you like to have your fate in his hands? You know we don't get along, we never have. And now Strong Arms is going to be messing around in my life, butting into things that aren't any of his business."

"He's better than you give him credit for," Alex said. "The man's come a long way."

Mor put both hands on his friend's shoulders. "Listen, you've got to promise me you'll look into this. Armstrong depends on you, Alex. He'll listen to your suggestions; he's done it in the past. Don't let him railroad me."

Alex had never seen his friend so intense. "I'll do what I can," Alex promised, wondering how he always seemed to get sucked into the sheriff's investigations. This was different, though; there was no way he could say no to his best friend in the world. If Mor needed him, Alex would be there, no questions asked.

He just hoped he would be able to help.

Alex walked over to Emma and Elise, with Mor close behind him. Alex said, "Emma, I know this isn't the greatest time to ask you questions, but did you have any idea your ex-husband was coming to Elkton Falls?"

"I never dreamed he'd come here," Emma said. "That part of my life was over." Did she avert her eyes as she answered him?

Alex pushed her harder. "Emma, this is important. You've got to tell me the truth."

Mor said firmly, "Alex, she's just had the shock of her life. Take it easy on her."

Alex said, "The sheriff is going to ask her the same questions I'm asking. I'm just trying to get to the bottom of this before he gets here."

Elise said, "She didn't kill him, Alex."

Emma put a hand on her arm. "It's all right, Elise, I know Alex just wants to help." She dabbed at her eyes with a handkerchief, then said, "The way I'm carrying on, you'd think I still loved the man, but I stopped being anything but afraid of Toby Sturbridge a long time ago. He was a horrid husband, and it wasn't just the violence, though that was bad enough. Toby gambled our money away faster than I could earn it, and he owed some really bad people. It's hard to say who I was more frightened of during the last years of our marriage, my husband or the loan sharks who used to come around to the house looking for him." She waved her handkerchief in the air like a white flag, then added, "It was just the shock of seeing him like that. I know I must sound like a monster, but truth be told, I'm glad he's gone. The man's been haunting my nightmares for years. All his bad karma finally came back for him, and I can't honestly say I'm sorry."

Alex said, "Emma, the sheriff's going to ask you about your relationship with him, things you thought were buried in your past. Be ready for his questions."

She seemed to stiffen her spine. "Alex, I've done nothing wrong. The only fault I had was staying with a man like that as long as I did."

Alex said, "You know Armstrong. He's going to stay after you until he's satisfied you're telling the truth."

He saw Emma flinch, and on a hunch, Alex asked again, "You didn't know he was here, did you, Emma?"

"Alex, that's enough," Elise snapped as Mor started to speak himself. There was a thunderous expression on the big man's face that Alex knew was a precursor to the storm sure to follow.

Before he could say anything, Emma said in a hoarse voice, "I'm sorry. You're right, I knew he was here. He asked me for money, demanded it from me, and threatened me if I didn't give it to him." She turned to her brand-new fiancé and said, "Mor, I didn't tell you because I was hoping he'd just go away." She turned back to Alex and said, "Is there a chance in the world the sheriff's going to believe me?"

Alex said, "I honestly don't know, but you have to tell him the truth. All of it."

Sheriff Armstrong was going to have a field day with Emma's blunt honesty and her confession that she knew her ex-husband was in town. Alex knew who Armstrong's two prime suspects were going to be: the battered ex-wife and her fiancé. It was going to take his best efforts to stop the sheriff from focusing on Emma and Mor and persuade him to look for the real killer.

The thought, however brief, flickered through his mind that maybe one of them had in fact had something to do with Sturbridge's death. Emma had every right to wish ill of the man, he had been a nasty bully from all accounts, and Alex knew from past experience how protective Mor was of anyone and anything he loved. Was it possible one of his friends could have committed murder?

If Mor thought he was protecting Emma, Alex was afraid the answer to that question wasn't going to be all that easy to uncover.

Sheriff Armstrong came flying up Point Road in his cruiser with the siren blaring and lights flashing. More than anything in the world, the sheriff loved to show the folks of Elkton Falls that he was on the job. Armstrong had nearly lost his last election for sheriff, and Alex had been surprised to find the man taking his work much more seriously, though the sheriff hadn't been able to break his ingrained habit of announcing his presence whenever there was a crime. Armstrong was actually turning into a pretty decent law enforcement officer, but he still needed a nudge in the right direction now and then, and Fate had appointed Alex to push.

Alex and Mor walked out onto the porch as the squad car approached. Emma and Elise had declined to join them. Just as well, Alex thought. There would be plenty of time for questions later.

Alex saw the sheriff's cousin and Canawba County's chief forensics expert, Irene Wilkins, in the front seat beside Armstrong. She must have had an opening in her schedule as Elkton Falls' resident beauty parlor operator. Irene was no lightweight when it came to crime scene investigation, she'd won several awards for her forensic work, but it was the fact that she kept Armstrong in line that Alex admired most about her. One "Ducky" from her, and all the puffed hot air shot right out of the sheriff. Irene was definitely not a book to be judged by its cover. Looking at her teased hair and listening to her brash manner, it was sometimes too easy to forget that she'd aced every class she'd taken in forensics, and was building up such a strong reputation that even many of her peers were grudgingly calling her in to consult on some of their tougher cases.

Armstrong shut off his lights and siren as he pulled up beside Mor's truck, now deserted in the field that had served as overflow parking behind the Main Keeper's Quarters. Alex and Mor reached them just as Armstrong's door opened.

The sheriff said, "Doc Drake's on his way," as he heaved himself out of the cruiser. Armstrong's steady politicking at Buck's Grill was apparent from his massive girth.

"Hello, boys," Irene said as she collected her investigation kit from the backseat of the squad car.

Armstrong asked Mor, "First thing I need to know is, did you move or touch anything?"

Mor said tersely, "It's my truck, Armstrong. My fingerprints are bound to be all over it."

Armstrong said, "Don't get your tail in a knot, Pendleton, I need to ask these questions. Now let me ask you again, did you touch the body or anything around it?"

Mor said, "I pulled him back to see if he was still alive. He was colder than January when I touched him, though."

Armstrong nodded toward the body. "And you said you recognized him right off the bat?"

"I told you on the phone, I've never seen him before in my life," Mor said. "When Emma told me who he was, I didn't believe her at first."

Armstrong nodded as Irene joined them with her video camera. There was no nonsense in Irene's voice as she said, "Excuse me, gentlemen, but I need some room to work. After I shoot the video, I want to take some Polaroid shots, then I'll get down to the close work."

As the three men stepped well away from the vehicle,

Armstrong said, "I'm going to need to talk to Emma Sturbridge. Either of you have any idea where she's at?"

Mor blocked the way back to the building. "Hang on a second. She's just had a real shock. Give her some time to get herself together, will you?"

Armstrong shook his head. "I'm going to do my best not to upset her, Mor, but it's real important I talk to her as soon as I can."

"I said you're going to have to wait." There was steel in Mor's voice as he stood his ground.

Armstrong took a deep breath, then said, "You need to think long and hard about interfering with this investigation, Mor. Now I know better than anybody that the two of us have never really gotten along, but that doesn't rightly matter at the moment. I've got a job to do, and I'm going to do it; you can bet your last hat on that." Armstrong paused, looked hard into Mor's eyes, and added, "It can go hard on you if you mess with me. I'm not trying to throw my weight around here, but I am going to speak with her, whether you like it or not."

Alex said, "He's right, Mor. The sheriff's just doing his job."

Mor argued, "I still say she's in no shape to talk with anybody."

"Well, she's talking to me," Armstrong said flatly.

Mor shook his head. "Not until she's talked to a lawyer. I know how you are, Armstrong. The likeliest suspect is the only person you focus on, and I won't have you putting Emma under your microscope. You have any questions, you can ask me."

Armstrong, finally letting his anger show, said, "The honest truth is that right now I've got two chief suspects, and you're one of them. You want me to start with you, you've got it. Let's go, big man."

Alex asked, "Where are you taking him?"

Armstrong said, "Irene's got the crime scene covered. I figured it might be easier to talk down at my office where we won't be disturbed. You don't mind coming along, do you, Mor?"

"Believe it or not, Sheriff, I want this killer caught just as much as you do. Just leave Emma alone."

Armstrong said softly, "Mor, you're going to have to stop telling me how to do my job. Emma will get her turn, and there's not a thing in the world you can do about that. Now go get in the backseat of the cruiser. I'll be right there."

Mor did as he was told, looking back at Alex as he opened the door. "Tell Emma where I went. And call Sandra for me, would you? Have her meet me at the sheriff's office."

Alex saw Armstrong grimace at the mention of Elkton Falls' most aggressive female lawyer. Alex and Sandra had dated off and on until Elise had come to the Hatteras West Inn, changing things between them forever. It had amazed Alex to discover that Sandra was a much better friend than girlfriend, once they got over their shared past. She was the perfect choice when someone he knew was in trouble with the law, especially since he'd lost his uncle Jase.

"I'll call her the second I get inside," Alex said as Armstrong started for the squad car.

The sheriff looked over his shoulder and said, "I couldn't talk you into forgetting her number for a while, could I?"

Alex said, "Sorry, but I can't do that, Sheriff."

Armstrong nodded. "I know that, I was half-joking. You can't blame me for trying, though." The sheriff paused, then added, "Alex, I know Mor and Emma are your best friends in the world, but I've got to do my job. Right now, whether you like it or not, they are my likeliest suspects."

Alex nodded. "I understand what you're saying, but I can't believe either one of them killed Sturbridge."

Armstrong said, "Let's just hope you're right. If you are, after I talk to both of them, I can go after the real killer." The sheriff called out to Irene, deeply immersed in her videotaping, "Give me a ring when you're ready to come back to town and I'll come pick you up."

Irene waved a hand toward him. "I'm done for the day at the shop, so take your time. I've got a good hour of work left to do here." Almost to herself, Irene said as she panned the camera, "I can't believe all these footprints. It looks like a marching band came through here."

Armstrong nodded to his cousin, then said, "See you later, Alex."

After the squad car pulled away, Alex asked Irene, "Can you tell what happened to him?"

Irene said, "Alex, you know I can't discuss any of this with you."

He said, "Sorry, I know how seriously you take your work. I respect that."

"And you're not going to get anything out of me by buttering me up, either," she said with a smile as she zoomed in on a particular footprint. "Why don't you go make that call Mor asked you to? 'Ducky' can get carried away when Sandra's not around to slap his hand."

"I'll do just that," Alex said as he hurried back to the inn.

As he walked back to the Dual Keepers' Quarters, Alex realized things were going to be a lot tougher on him than they used to be. Now that both buildings were reopened for guests, Alex's penchant for investigation was going to be curtailed greatly. It was one thing skipping out on a handful of guests now and then to track down leads, but with two full buildings, it was going to take nearly all of his time and energy to run the inn, even with Elise's extensive help. She'd added a continental breakfast to their plan, which made more money for the inn, but also created more work, though Sally Anne from Buck's Grill brought out the muffins and fruit after the diner closed each night or before they opened the next day, depending on Sally Anne's schedule. Maybe Alex could recruit her to keep a watchful eye in town, since just about all of Elkton Falls passed through Buck's doors every day. He'd make it a point to talk to Sally Anne when she made her next delivery to the inn. Perhaps she could somehow help him prove that his best friends were innocent of murder.

Turning Mor down hadn't even been an option in his mind. Alex was going to have to do something. He'd given Mor his word, and that was something never to be taken lightly. Somehow Alex was just going to have to make the time. Who needed sleep, anyway?

As Alex walked into the lobby, Emma kept looking behind him. "Where's Mor? Why isn't he with you?"

Alex said gently, "The sheriff decided to talk to him down at his office." He saw Emma's face go white, so he added quickly, "He just wanted to interview him without all the distractions of Irene's investigation out here."

Emma said stonily, "I'm the one he should be talking to, not Mor. This is all my fault."

Elise said, "You had no control over your ex-husband. We all know that." She tried to smile, but had a difficult time doing it as she added, "Don't worry, Emma. Mor's a big boy, he can take care of himself."

Alex said, "Speaking of which, Mor asked me to call Sandra. Just as a precaution."

Elise nodded absently. "Of course." The two women had an uneasy truce when it came to Alex, but Elise knew as well as everyone else in town that Sandra was the one to call when there was real trouble.

Sandra's new secretary, Gretel Hanson, picked up on the first ring. The second she realized who was calling, Gretel asked breathlessly, "Alex, is it true? They found another body at your inn? You're going to have more ghosts than guests if this keeps up." She was obviously tickled by her wordplay.

Ignoring the barb, Alex asked, "Gretel, is Sandra free? I really need to talk to her."

"Let me check," Gretel said, and a minute later Sandra came on the line.

She said, "I just got off the phone with Mor, if that's what you're calling about. How bizarre is that, finding Emma's ex in the front seat of his truck at the inn?"

"I know, it doesn't look good for either of my friends. Are you going to help him?"

Sandra said, "I'll do what I can. Armstrong's just interviewing witnesses right now, but Mor thought I should sit in on the session. I'm on my way over there the second we hang up. Is Emma Sturbridge still at the inn?"

"She's right here," Alex admitted.

"Put her on, would you?"

Alex did as he was told. After a hushed conversation, Emma hung up the telephone. "Sandra thinks I should go on over to the jail and talk to the Sheriff as soon as he's done with Mor. She said she'd sit in on my questioning too, if I wanted her to. What do you two think?"

Elise said, "I think it's a good idea, just to be on the safe side."

Alex added, "I couldn't agree more. Would you like one of us to drive you? You probably shouldn't be alone right now."

Emma said, "I'll be fine. I've got my car. I met Mor here for the Grand Unveiling, and he'll need a ride home." She waved her handkerchief in the air. "Besides, you two have an inn to run. What have you got, one room empty in the entire place? You're going to have plenty on your plate as it is."

Alex said, "Our friends come first, Emma, you know that."

She started to tear up again, but nipped it off quickly. "You two are so special to us both. I've got to go."

Elise said, "Give us a call when you're finished with the sheriff, will you? Emma, we believe in you."

"Thanks so much," she said as she hurried out the door.

After Emma was gone, Elise turned to Alex and asked, "So what do you think really happened to Toby Sturbridge?"

"I wish I knew," he replied, staring out the window as Emma's car headed out Point Road.

At that moment, the house phone rang, and as Alex moved to answer his guest's summons, he wondered what the truth really was surrounding Toby Sturbridge's untimely demise.

3

As Alex hung up the house telephone after a brief conversation with one of their guests, Elise asked, "Is there anything I can do?"

"No, it was Lenora MacLeod in Room 7. She wants to talk to me."

Elise said, "If you don't need me, I'm going to go over and finish up next door at Main."

"I'll be over as soon as I can to help," Alex said.

"I've got it covered, there's really not that much left to do. After you take care of Ms. MacLeod, why don't you go see if you can pry anything else out of Irene?"

"She's being pretty tightlipped about everything," Alex said.

Elise smiled slightly. "Come on, Alex, you aren't trying hard enough. Turn on that Winston charm."

Alex said, "I would, but I'm saving it all for Saturday night. We're still on, aren't we?"

"I won't back out if you won't," Elise said steadily.

Alex pretended to ponder just that, then smiled brightly. "Not a chance."

As Elise left for the other building, Alex watched her

walk away. He was still savoring the warmth of their exchange when Lenora MacLeod walked in, a sketch pad tucked under one arm. Lenora was a striking woman in her late twenties, with long blond hair and hazel eyes, though no one would call her beautiful. There was something about her, though, a bold confidence and assurance, that was almost magnetic.

She said, "Alex? Is this a bad time?"

"No, Ma'am. What can I do for you?"

"When I first arrived, you promised me a personal tour of your lighthouse. I was hoping you could take me to the observation platform and show me the mountains."

Alex glanced at his watch. He had indeed promised her a guided tour, but this wasn't the greatest time to leave the front desk.

Lenora caught his expression. "If now is not convenient for you, perhaps we could schedule it for sometime later," she said, letting her words trail softly away.

"No, now is fine." He was an innkeeper first and foremost, and this was definitely part of his job. Alex put up a sign that said BACK IN THIRTY MINUTES, then led Lenora out the door. Doc Drake still hadn't arrived on the scene, so Alex still had plenty of time to act as a tour guide to one of his guests.

As they climbed the steel staircase inside the lighthouse, Lenora let her fingers trail along the whitewashed wall inside the tower. "Such fine character it has."

"I like to think so. It's been a part of my family for generations."

"It is a part of you as well, Alex. I can feel it in you both." Her words were spoken like a declaration.

Alex said, "I can't deny it. After all, I was born at the bottom of these steps."

Lenora said, "Would you tell me the story as we climb?"

It was a good thing Alex made it a point to climb the steps on a regular basis. Otherwise he wouldn't have had the spare breath to talk on their ascent. Lenora must have been in great shape; the climb didn't seem to faze her at all.

Alex said, "It was on a Halloween night thirty-odd years ago. Hurricane Abby took a freak turn and headed up through Charlotte, then Hickory, and finally straight through Elkton Falls. My mother was nine months pregnant with me, but she refused to evacuate. I don't doubt Dad realized from the start that getting her to leave was not a battle he could win. Anyway, her water broke about the time the first edge of the storm hit, and he delivered me himself right here."

"I would think your family would head for a basement, not a tower, in a hurricane."

Alex said, "Hatteras West is nearly an exact replica of the Cape Hatteras Lighthouse on the Outer Banks. These lighthouses were built to withstand the punishment of the storms."

They ascended to the top, and Lenora gasped as she took in the views of the mountains in one direction and the foothills in the other. It was breathtaking at the top, a view Alex could never grow tired of. He only wished there was a fog rolling in for Lenora's visit. It was truly spectacular watching the bands of gentle whiteness engulf the land below while staying high above it all.

After naming several of the nearby mountain ridges, Alex saw Doc Drake's car pull up beside Mor's truck below them.

"Lenora, there's something I need to take care of. Are you interested in coming back down with me?"

She shook her head. "I want to stay up here and soak this all in, perhaps do a few sketches. You go ahead, Alex. Thank you for the tour."

"My pleasure. If there's anything else I can do to make your stay a more pleasurable one, just let me know."

She smiled slightly, more in her eyes than her lips. Lenora said, "There will come a time when I do just that, but it is not here yet."

Now what in the world did that mean? "Just let me know," Alex said as he jogged back down the steps.

He didn't want Drake to get out of there without giving him a clue as to what exactly had killed Toby Sturbridge.

* * *

An ambulance had pulled up behind the doctor's car as Alex trotted down the steps, and Drake was already in the process of examining the body slumped behind Mor's steering wheel when he caught up with him.

Doc Drake was a wiry little man with more energy than four normal folks. There was a look of intense focus on his face as he concentrated on the body.

Alex asked over the doctor's shoulder, "Any luck yet?"

Drake shook his head, still partially inside the truck examining the body. Irene stood nearby, filming the examination for her own records. She said, "Step back, Alex, could you? You're blocking my shot." What the eye might miss, Irene would have on tape.

After his preliminary examination, Drake muttered, "I can tell you this, there's nothing all that obvious that just jumps out at me."

He started shaking his head as he kept looking, checking the eyes, the rigidity of the body, and a dozen other things Alex couldn't begin to interpret.

Finally, Drake said to the two attendants waiting nearby, "Okay, let's take him out of the cab."

As they gently eased the body out of the truck, Irene zoomed in for a closer look. It wasn't work for the faint-hearted, that was certain.

After Sturbridge was on the stretcher, Drake gave the body a more thorough examination. Finally, he raised his head and made eye contact with Alex. "If you want my professional opinion, I don't have a clue. There are no obvious signs of trauma, at least nothing I can find out here. Alex, it could have been a dozen things, including natural causes. I need to get him to the hospital and take a closer look."

Irene had vanished, and Alex saw her zooming in on something under Mor's front seat. He looked and spotted a dozen red roses pushed under the seat.

Irene said, "I wonder if these were from Mor, or from old Toby over there."

Alex said, "I don't have any idea. Is there a card with

them?" He started to bend down to get a better look when he heard tires crunching on the gravel drive nearby.

Sheriff Armstrong was back, and for a man of his bulk, he joined them with astonishing speed.

"What's going on?" he asked, fighting to catch his breath.

"We just found something," Alex said.

Armstrong said, "Alex, why don't you leave this to the professionals? I'll come find you when we're done and bring you up to speed." He forgot about Alex instantly and turned back to Irene. "Now show me what you've got."

Alex stepped back a few paces, but he wasn't about to leave. After all, whatever had happened to Emma's ex-husband had happened at Hatteras West on Winston land, and he had a right to know what was going on.

Alex glanced over and saw the body being quickly loaded into the ambulance as Doc Drake headed for his car.

Alex caught him before he could drive away. "Are you still stumped?"

Drake admitted, "They're not all as obvious as a knife wound in the back of the neck, Alex. This one's going to take a little time."

Alex asked softly, "Doc, give me a call when you find anything, will you?"

Drake said, "Did you know the man, Alex? What's your interest in this case?"

"He's Emma Sturbridge's ex-husband, and she and Mor are most likely going to be the sheriff's main suspects. Besides, this happened on my land. I feel responsible for it."

Drake thought about it for a few moments, then said, "I'll see what I can do, but I'm not making any promises." As Drake got into his car, he added, "You know how the sheriff gets when you snoop, Alex."

Armstrong tried to catch the doctor's attention before he could leave, but Drake was deep in conversation on his cellular phone as he drove away.

"Blast it all, I was expecting a report," the sheriff said.

Alex replied, "He doesn't know anything yet, just that there's no obvious trauma."

Armstrong said, "Alex, I don't like hearing it second-hand from you. I told you before, I don't want you getting involved in this."

"I'm not sure I'm going to be able to oblige you, Sheriff. Your two main suspects are both my friends."

Armstrong said, "I'm not so sure that buys you a ticket to the dance. Tell me the truth. Mor asked you to poke around in this, didn't he?"

"He might have mentioned it," Alex admitted reluctantly.

Armstrong shook his head. "He's going to make this a hundred times harder than it has to be, I just know it. He's already screaming about bringing in the State Police, and we don't even know for sure what happened out here today."

"Is he still in custody?" Alex asked warily.

"He was *never* in custody," the sheriff protested. "I wouldn't even have bothered taking him downtown if he hadn't goaded me into it with that grandstanding of his. You know, if I didn't know any better, I'd say he was doing it to protect Emma."

Alex felt the relief flood through him. "So he's not one of your suspects, then."

"First why don't we let Doc Drake figure out exactly what happened to the man before we start lining up suspects. There will be plenty of time to worry about who did what after that. For right now, though, Emma and Mor are free to go about their business, just as long as they don't plan to take any trips out of town."

Alex said, "They're getting married in a month. I'm guessing they'll be taking a honeymoon right after that. Most folks do."

"Truth be told, if I don't have this wrapped up in a month, I might not be able to stop them, but I'm going to try."

"Are you at least finished with Mor's truck? He won't

be able to work without it." Mor, along with his partner Les Williamson, owned and operated Mor or Les, Elkton Falls' premier handyman service.

"I have half a mind to impound it, he's being such a thorn in my side. But I'm not about to do that," the sheriff added, killing the protest just breaking Alex's lips. Armstrong called out to Irene, "How much more time do you need with the truck?"

Irene considered the question for a few moments, then said, "I could do a better, more thorough job if I had it in the police garage. Get a tow truck, Ducky, and let's haul it in."

Alex protested, "Is that really necessary? I mean, you always do a good job in the field."

Irene said, "I've got the time to be thorough, Alex. Mrs. Harper cancelled her perm appointment, so I'm free the rest of the day."

Armstrong said, "Irene, you don't have to justify your request to Alex. You want Mor's truck towed in, then that's the way it's going to be." He saw someone driving up to them and said, "Now what's the mayor doing out here at this time of day?"

Grady got out of his car and approached them. "Hi all. I was out this way running an errand, so I thought I'd come by and see if you've made any progress yet."

Armstrong said, "I've got my crew hard at work on it."

Grady nodded to Irene. "Ma'am."

"Mr. Mayor."

Armstrong said, "I told you, as soon as we've come up with something, I'll let you know."

Grady nodded, then patted Alex's shoulder. "So, have you thought any more about going into politics?"

Alex said, "No, sir, I've got my hands full just being an innkeeper."

Grady said, "You can do both, Alex." He started back for his car, then said, "Talk to you all later."

After the mayor drove off, Armstrong headed to his squad car to call for a tow truck on his radio.

Alex said, "Irene, do you really have to tow Mor's truck into town?"

Irene said, "This will save Mor a trip out to the inn. He can walk over to the police garage and pick it up in an hour."

Alex nodded. "I never thought about that. Irene, I'm not asking you to put your neck on the line, but do you have *any* idea what happened?"

"A man died, Alex, that's all I can say. Don't worry, we'll know more soon enough."

After the tow truck came and hauled Mor's truck off, there was no reason for Irene or the sheriff to hang around Hatteras West. They got back into the cruiser and Alex watched them drive away.

He couldn't imagine what Irene might find upon taking a closer look at the truck.

Alex just hoped if anything did turn up, it wouldn't point to either of his two friends.

Alex was back at the main desk trying to get a handle on having a full house of guests again when he looked up from the inn's registry to find the two ladies sharing Room 16 approach.

He greeted them with his best innkeeper's smile, then said, "Good afternoon, Ladies. We were beginning to worry about you."

Corki stifled a yawn as she admitted, "To be honest with you, we've needed our rest. I never imagined this tour of inns would be so exhausting."

Jan added, "I never worked so hard in my life as we did at that place in Pennsylvania. Magdalena nearly wore us out with that true Amish experience."

Alex smiled softly to himself. He'd met Magdalena Yoder years before at an innkeepers affair, and she'd bragged about her penchant for keeping her guests busy with chores, even paying for the privilege. Alex wished wistfully that he'd have the nerve to do that himself.

Well, it was worth a shot. Alex said, "If you two decide

you want to get the authentic Lighthouse Experience, I've got plenty of rags and cleaners, and the glass around the lens could use a good scrubbing."

Corki held her palms up in the air. "No more work for me. All I want to do is eat and sleep. I'm ready for a real vacation."

Jan chimed in, "Absolutely. Alex, we came down for directions to Mama Ravolini's. We've heard great things about the restaurant. Is it far?"

Alex took out a highlighter and traced the route on a photocopied map of Elkton Falls for the ladies. As he handed the sheet to them, Corki said, "Don't wait up. We're going to see every bit of nightlife Elkton Falls has to offer."

As the two women drove away, Alex knew they'd most likely be back before he extinguished the lobby fire for the night at 10 P.M. Elkton Falls just wasn't all that exciting in the evening, and honestly, that was one of the things he loved about living in the small town.

Alex was ready to call it a night when a couple in their thirties came crashing into the inn.

The woman was hounding the man even as they burst through the door. "I told you this was it, Paul. 'Follow the lighthouse,' you said. 'We're bound to get there sooner or later,' you said. If that farmer hadn't given us directions, we'd still be driving around in circles."

"Sheila, if you think you can do better next time, you drive. At least then you won't be on my back about the directions."

Alex asked, "May I help you?"

"We want the Main Keeper's Suite. That's the best room you've got in the old building, isn't it?" the woman barked out.

"I'm sorry, but that room is reserved for the next two weeks."

Sheila turned to the man beside her and said, "I told you

we should have called ahead. But no, you were sure it would be vacant."

Paul protested, "Hey, the reservations were your job. Don't lay this one on me. I can't do everything."

As they caught their breaths before starting in on each other again, Alex said, "We do have one room available, but I'm afraid it's not in this building at all. It's in the Dual Keepers' Quarters over there." He pointed through the window to the building next door.

"It's brand new, isn't it," the woman said disdainfully.

"Bright and shining. In fact, this is the first night it's officially open."

"So much for our historic honeymoon," the woman snapped at her spouse.

The man stepped forward and said to Alex in a low voice, "Listen, I know this is late notice, but couldn't you do a little shuffling for us? I can make it worth your while." As he made his request, he slid a hundred-dollar bill across the counter.

Alex refused to touch the bill. "I'm truly sorry, but I can't help you. Mrs. Nesbitt reserves that same room every year. If you think you'd be happier elsewhere, there are quite a few places in Hickory to stay, and it's not that far away."

The woman shouldered her way past her new husband and said, "I'm sure whatever you have here will be fine."

Alex nodded. "Good enough. I just need you to sign in and we'll get you settled. Will this be cash or charge?"

The woman retrieved the hundred and slipped it into her purse as she said, "Pay the man, Paul. Put it on your credit card."

He obviously wanted to protest, but one look at his glaring bride told him this was not a battle worth fighting.

As Paul filled out the registration, his bride said, "I'm going to go look at the lighthouse. Come get me when you're ready." As she went out onto the porch, Alex heard her mutter, "That's just wonderful. It's not even lit up."

Alex offered to lead the way to their room after they'd

settled the billing, but the man refused his aid. "I can handle it from here."

"Good night, then, Mr. Jones."

"Good night." As he walked out, Alex heard Jones say under his breath, "Man oh man. What have I gotten myself into?"

4

Sally Anne came in with a basket of fresh muffins for the next day's breakfast just as Alex was about to douse the fire in the lobby and head off to bed. Corki and Jan had returned hours ago and were tucked safely in, along with the other guests of the Hatteras West Inn. Elise was in the middle of reading Carl Sandburg's *Lincoln*, a set of volumes Alex had inherited from his late uncle Jase, and she'd left him earlier for the privacy of her room. Was it his imagination, or was there a new awkwardness surrounding them now that their first date was nearly upon them? Alex had to admit, he was a little hesitant to meddle with their friendship and working relationship by throwing romance into the mix, but the pull he felt for her was too strong to ignore.

No matter what happened between them, he had to know one way or another, once and for all, if there was a chance for romance with her.

Sally Anne set down the basket and said, "You look like you've got the world's troubles on your shoulders, Alex."

He said, "No, I'm just trying to put a few things in perspective."

Sally Anne nodded. "I heard about Emma's ex showing up here dead. Do they know what happened yet?"

Alex said, "I figured you'd have a better handle on that than I would. Your diner is a pretty popular place with the sheriff and everybody else in town."

"It's funny, but we haven't seen Armstrong since he got the call to come out here. Dad's worried he's starving himself to death," she added with a grin.

As Alex paid Sally Anne's bill, he said, "I've got a question for you. How'd you like to be my eyes in town?"

"You mean like a spy?" Sally Anne asked eagerly.

"More of an observer," Alex said. When he saw her smile dim, he added, "Okay, to be honest with you, it's exactly like a spy."

Sally Anne said, "How cool. Just tell me what you want me to do."

"Right now, I need you to keep your eyes and ears open around the diner. I promised Mor I'd look into Sturbridge's death, and I'm going to need your help in town now that both of my buildings are full."

Sally Anne said, "I was kind of hoping there'd be more skulking around."

Alex laughed. "I'll see what I can come up with. Seriously, you don't mind helping me?"

"Alex, since I lost my fiancé to the Carolina football program and those perky cheerleaders they have there, I've got way too much time on my hands. This sounds like fun." She paused, then added, "If it's all the same to you though, I don't think I'm going to tell Dad. He's kind of overprotective of me."

"Don't lie to him on my account," Alex said, though he suddenly realized getting on Buck's bad side might not be the smartest move, especially since the man was a former Golden Gloves boxer who still kept in shape by assaulting a punching bag in his basement.

Sally Anne said, "Oh, he's a pussycat, Alex. Besides, he really likes you."

Alex said, "Let's make sure we keep it that way. Thanks for helping, Sally Anne."

"My pleasure."

Elise came out of her room and said, "I thought I heard voices out here."

Sally Anne said, "Hey, Elise. I was just leaving."

"Not on my account, I hope," Elise said.

"No, Dad's waiting in the car." She headed for the door and called out, "Bye now," as she left.

Elise looked at the basket, then said, "I wasn't eavesdropping, but did I hear you ask Sally Anne to help you with your snooping?"

"We're going to have our hands full with our guests now that both buildings are at full capacity again, so I asked her to keep an eye on what's going on around town."

Elise said, "I've been meaning to talk to you about that. Are you sure our date Saturday night is such a good idea? Someone should be here for our guests all the time."

A chill crept into Alex's heart. "Elise, are you having second thoughts about going out with me?"

She said, "Of course not." Then, after hesitating, she added, "Why, are you?"

Alex took her hands in his and said, "I know this is a big step for us, but don't you think it's time we found out exactly what this is between us?"

Elise pulled away. "Alex, I don't want to lose your friendship. I've got plenty of ex-boyfriends, but you're the only best friend I've got."

Alex sighed. "Okay, so we'll make a pact. If it doesn't work out between us, we'll stay friends, no matter what." He added with a grin, "Besides, we'll have to be, since we see each other every day."

Elise said, "You say that now, but what happens if it ends badly?"

Alex thought about it a moment, then said, "Elise, I'd rather take that chance than miss out on something that could be the best thing that ever happened to me."

Alex wasn't sure what he expected her reaction to be to his statement, but seeing her bolt to her room was not one of the possibilities he would have considered. Shaking his head, Alex finished his nightly closing duties, made a quick tour through both buildings, then walked out onto the porch of the Main Keeper's Quarters.

The lighthouse looked down at him, its lens darkened by the night. He was tempted to turn it on, despite what the Elkton Falls Town Council thought. It was a beacon that was made to be lit.

With a mischievous grin, Alex decided to do it anyway. After grabbing a flashlight, he headed up the tower's steps. Just a few brief seconds of light surely couldn't hurt anything.

As his hand reached for the plain button switch his grandfather had installed, Alex felt a flutter of anticipation in his stomach. He never got tired of lighting the beacon.

When he pushed the button though, nothing happened. The old switch had finally died. He'd have to call Mor in the morning and have him take a look at it. Though Alex had the nominal skills to fix lots of things around the inn in a pinch, he normally left the electrical work to Mor. Disappointed that the light wouldn't shine that night, Alex walked out onto the observation platform, playing his flashlight over the railing as he walked. Once he was securely in place, he turned off his light and looked out in the vast darkness around him. It took nearly fifteen minutes for his eyes to grow accustomed to the darkness. In the stillness of the night, the sounds around him were intensified and amplified. It was one of the many reasons he loved the lighthouse so much. The beacon had more shifting moods and facets than most folks ever suspected.

The next morning, Alex found Elise setting up their continental breakfast bar for their guests, with fresh coffee, orange juice, and the supplies Sally Anne had dropped off the night before. The bar added to their expenses, but with the accompanying room rate increase, they actually made more profit off each guest who came to Hatteras West. It was one of Elise's touches Alex liked so much, providing a nice service while raising their revenues at the same time.

"That smells good," he said.

"The coffee?" Elise asked. "I'd be glad to get you a cup."

"You know me better than that. I like the smell, not the taste. So when are we going to start offering sweet tea with our little spread here?"

"Whenever you want to get up early and make it," Elise said, teasing.

"You're in a good mood today," Alex said.

"I always wake up happy, you know that."

Alex said, "I do. We know each other's patterns pretty well, don't we?"

Elise said softly, "So all the mystery's gone, is that what you're trying to say?"

Alex laughed softly. "Just the opposite. I'm looking forward to seeing more of you than I already have."

"Not on the first date, you won't," Elise said.

Alex stammered, "That's not what I meant. I was . . . What I meant to say . . ."

She finally took pity on him and snapped him lightly with a tea towel she had used for the muffins. "You can stop squirming, I know exactly what you meant."

Alex was about to say something else when Lenora walked in. "That coffee smells like ambrosia."

"Help yourself," Alex said.

As she poured a cup and selected a blueberry muffin, Lenora said, "Alex, I was hoping you had some spare time this morning. I really need to speak with you."

"Sorry, I don't normally have any free time until around lunch," Alex said. "We keep pretty busy till then." He and Elise worked at their housekeeping chores together in the mornings, though they would probably have to adjust their schedules now that they were running two separate buildings.

"That will be fine. May I treat you to a meal at this Buck's Grill I keep hearing about?"

"No need. We can go Dutch," he said.

"Ah, but then I can't ask you my favor. I'll meet you here at noon."

After she was gone, Elise said, "I know it's none of my business, but what exactly was that all about?"

"I don't have the slightest idea. But hey, how can I say no to a free lunch?"

"Well, you could always try 'no'. Then there's 'no thank you', 'sorry I can't' and the old reliable 'no Ma'am, but I appreciate you thinking of me'. Any of those would work."

Alex said, "It's just lunch, and she *is* our guest. Besides, I've got to admit, this whole 'favor' thing she's been dropping hints about has me intrigued. I can't imagine what she wants."

Elise cocked her head to one side, then said, "No doubt that's her intent. Don't worry, I'm sure you'll find out soon enough."

The bickering honeymoon couple joined them, filled their plates and mugs, then grabbed a table away from everyone else, presumably so they could have some privacy.

Alex asked Elise, "So, should we keep tag teaming the rooms together, or should we split up now that we have so much ground to cover?"

Elise said, "Tell you what. You take Main and I'll handle Dual. We can do the sheets after lunch together, if you get back from your rendezvous in time."

Alex said, "I'll be here. You know, it's going to be kind of odd doing the rooms alone again."

"We've both gotten spoiled with the light workload. I'm afraid that's about to end."

"I've got a feeling you're right. Before I get started on my rooms, I've got to call Mor."

"Is it about Emma's ex-husband?"

Alex admitted sheepishly, "Actually, it's a handyman job. I tried to turn on the lens last night and the switch was broken."

Elise looked surprised by the admission. "I thought the Town Council banned you from doing that."

He said, "I don't know, all of a sudden I just had to see the light, fine or no fine."

Elise nodded. "I'm surprised the urge doesn't hit you more often. Do me a favor the next time you get the yen."

"What's that?"

"Come get me first. I would love to see the sky lit up again."

Alex smiled. "I promise."

It left things on a much better note as Elise headed off to start on Dual.

Mor picked up on the third ring when Alex called. "Mor or Les," he said automatically.

Alex said, "I thought you usually let Les answer the phone."

Mor said, "Believe me, it's not by choice. He's off visiting family in Florida, so for the next four days, I'm it. Has something happened with the case?"

Alex admitted, "I haven't heard a thing. How did your interview with the sheriff go?"

"Armstrong blustered around a little, then he set me loose after Sandra quit putting up with his foolishness. I don't know if he was just fishing, or if Sandra intimidated him, but we didn't cover much ground. I hung around until he finished with Emma. She was in there less time than I was. He told us to hang around Elkton Falls, but that was about it." Mor sighed. "Like I could just take off any time I wanted to with Les gone. So if you aren't calling about the case, what's up?"

"The light switch for the lens is broken, at least I think that's the problem, and I'd like you to take a look at it whenever you get the chance."

Mor said, "I know you don't have permission to fire it up, Alex. What's going on?"

He explained, "What's the use of having the world's biggest night-light if you can't turn it on now and then?"

Mor chuckled. "That's the spirit. I'll try to make it out there this evening."

"No hurry, you don't have to work at night on my account. I know you've got your hands full."

Mor said, "Think about it, Alex. You're allowed to perform regular testing and maintenance on the light since it serves as an early warning notice for the county, am I right? Why don't I show up tonight and we'll try out the new switch when we can enjoy it? I'll call Grady Hatch and tell him what we're doing."

"That sounds great," Alex said.

Suddenly, Tracy Shook rushed into the inn. There was a look of urgency on her face that required immediate attention.

Alex said, "I've got to go, Mor. See you tonight."

After he hung up with his friend, Alex said, "Tracy, what's going on? You look like you've seen a ghost."

"Alex, is the sheriff here?"

He said, "I haven't seen him all morning. You look upset, Tracy. What's wrong?"

"It's Oxford Hitchcock. He's disappeared."

"Slow down," Alex said. "What do you mean, he's disappeared?"

"We were supposed to speak at a dinner together last night for the Sons of the South, but he never showed up."

"So maybe he got his dates mixed up," Alex said. "It happens."

"That's his group, Alex, and he had the perfect opportunity to show me up. There's not a chance in the world he forgot about it. I went by his house last night after the banquet, but nobody was home. Then this morning we had a breakfast debate scheduled for Hal's radio show in Hickory, and I had to do it alone."

"I thought you'd be happy about the lack of competition," Alex said.

"This isn't funny. Oxford and I are competitors, but we're buddies too, no matter how much stress this campaign has put on our friendship. I'm worried something might have happened to him, so I've been looking for the sheriff. Maybe he can figure out what's going on."

"I'm sure it's nothing," Alex said.

"I wish I could believe that." She sighed, then added, "I've been putting it off, but I guess I'm going to have to call the snake and see if he knows where Oxford is."

Alex knew she must be really worried if she was willing to call her ex-husband. "What's his number? I'll give him a call for you."

Tracy said, "Thanks, Alex, I'd really appreciate that."

Alex dialed Conner's number, but after two rings, he got the answering machine.

After he hung up, Alex said, "He wasn't there, so I left a message for him to call me."

Tracy said, "Something's not right, Alex. His calls are forwarded to his cell phone when his home number doesn't answer. How many times did it ring before you got the machine?"

"Twice," Alex said. "Why?"

Tracy picked up the phone, and as she punched in the number, she said, "I just hope he hasn't changed the access code."

Her face went white as she listened intently.

"What was it?" Alex asked.

"Listen to this." Tracy punched another number, and Alex heard Oxford's voice in a near whisper on the recording. "Conner, I'm in real trouble here. I need . . ."

And then the message died before he had the chance to say another word.

5

Alex had her replay the message. After listening to it intently, he said, "Tracy, we both should probably forget we ever listened to this."

Tracy said, "Come on, you heard him, Alex. He's in trouble, and Conner wasn't there to help him. Not that I'm surprised, he was never there when I needed him either, but I can't ignore what I just heard."

Alex said, "We need to think about this before we do anything rash. What can the sheriff do, based on what we just heard?" A sudden thought crossed his mind. "Tracy, you could get in serious trouble if Armstrong finds out you checked your ex-husband's messages. It's invading his privacy. Even if you get away with it, the voters aren't going to be happy about it."

"I don't care about any of that. Oxford is in trouble."

Alex thought about it a full minute, then said, "Tracy, let me try to get the sheriff into this without involving you. And do me a favor, stay away from Conner's answering machine from now on. I can't see any way it's a good thing for you to be doing it."

She ignored his chiding and shook the receiver at him. "Call the sheriff, Alex."

He agreed, and dialed the sheriff's office. "He's at Buck's," Alex was told, so he called the Grill.

Armstrong came to the phone and said, "What's up, Alex? I was just getting a bowl of oatmeal, but it can wait. Find another body out there?"

"Bite your tongue," Alex said. "I was wondering if you might have seen Oxford Hitchcock around. He was supposed to come out by the inn this morning, but he never showed up," Alex lied.

"Hang on a second, Alex," Armstrong said. He must have put his hand over the phone to muffle his voice, but Alex could still hear as the sheriff asked the crowd at Buck's if anyone had seen the missing mayoral candidate.

Armstrong came back on the line a few seconds later and said, "Nope, he missed a meeting last night and one this morning, too. I wonder what he's up to."

Alex had to handle the next part delicately. "I wonder who else might know where he's at. Listen, if you see Oxford, give me a call, would you?"

The sheriff said, "Sure thing, Alex. Hey, hang on a second. Here comes Conner Shook. If anybody knows where Oxford is, he'll be the one."

Alex heard Armstrong ask, "Conner, you seen your candidate lately? He's missing appointments all over town."

Conner swore in the background, and Alex heard Buck say loudly, "I don't care if I am supporting your guy, there's no swearing allowed in here."

He heard Conner quickly apologize, then the campaign manager said, "I went to Charlotte on one overnight business trip and the man falls apart on me. Let me check my messages. The battery on my cell phone was nearly dead last night, so I had to recharge it on the road this morning."

There was a pause, and Alex knew what was coming next.

He heard Conner say, "Sheriff, you'd better listen to this."

Armstrong said, "Alex, I've got to go. I'll call you later."

When he hung up the telephone, Alex told Tracy, "Conner just showed up at the diner, and he checked his messages while I was on the line. Armstrong's right there, so they'll know what we know in a minute."

Tracy said, "Alex, I've got a bad feeling about this. It's just not like Oxford to vanish like this."

"Don't borrow trouble," Alex said. "I'm sure he's fine."

"I hope so," Tracy said as she started for the door. "Call me if you hear anything."

He said, "Only if you'll promise to do the same."

After Tracy was gone, Alex got out his cart and started cleaning the rooms. With all the interruptions, he was going to have to hustle if he was going to make his lunch date with Lenora, and as much as Alex was worried about what might have happened to Oxford Hitchcock, he could worry just as easily while he cleaned the rooms on his list.

"This is quite nice," Lenora said as they finished their lunch at Buck's. She'd carefully avoided all talk of the favor she wanted to ask him, and Alex was glad to leave it alone for the moment. There were more than a few raised eyebrows when folks around town saw him eating with a mysterious stranger, but no one said a word to him. Alex knew as soon as he and Lenora left, the rumors would start flying. It was part of living in a small town, putting up with the gossip of the lightning-quick kudzu vine.

Sally Anne brought the check to their table, and Lenora reached for it. As the inn's guest meted out the money, Sally Anne told Alex, "It's been quiet around here today since your phone call," the grin obvious on her face.

"I've got a feeling that's all about to change," Alex said.

Sally Anne took the money, winked at Alex, then walked away.

"Are you two involved in some way?" Lenora asked.

"Do you mean Sally Anne? No, we're just friends."

Lenora said softly, "Perhaps on your part. With her, it's not as clear."

Alex said, "You just don't know her. We've been joking around with each other since she was in braces and pigtails." Alex took a last sip of his sweet tea, then said, "We've had our lunch, and you still haven't asked your favor."

Lenora, sensing that Alex had shifted the conversation intentionally, acquiesced. "Very well. Alex, I want you to model for me."

Alex couldn't entirely bite back his laugh, and he looked sheepishly around as conversations all through Buck's paused to see what might happen next. "Sorry," Alex said in a lowered voice. "You caught me off guard with that one. Nobody's ever confused me with a model before."

Lenora said, "And why not? You have rich cheekbones, a noble nose, and a profile worth capturing on paper."

Alex didn't know what to say to that. "I thought you did landscapes. You were sketching at the top of the lighthouse yesterday, weren't you?"

"I work in my many mediums with a host of subjects, Alex. I would be most grateful if you would allow me to sketch you."

Alex said, "Lenora, I'm not sure I'm the right man for the job. There are a lot of better-looking folks in this world." He gestured around the room. "You probably wouldn't have a hard time finding one eating right here in Buck's."

Lenora shook her head. "Let me be the judge of that, Alex. It's you I want for my subject."

"Tell you what, let me sleep on it, okay?"

"I'll await your answer tomorrow morning," she agreed.

As Alex stood, he said, "Well, I have to get back to the inn if you're ready to go. Elise and I still have some laundry to do."

Lenora said, "I believe I'll stay here in town, if it's all the same to you. I'd like to get a feel for Elkton Falls.

Don't worry about my transportation back to the inn. I'll take a taxi."

Alex said, "Rebecca Gray has the only cab in town, but don't expect much. She uses her dad's pickup truck, and it's almost in worse shape than mine is. It's great for hauling luggage, but there's not a lot of passenger room up front."

Lenora just smiled. "This is why I love small towns."

"We have our moments," Alex said.

On the way back to Hatteras West, Alex thought about Lenora's offer. He considered himself passable in the looks department, but a model? No, it was too outlandish to even consider.

If he hurried, he'd be able to make it back to the inn before Elise got started on that laundry.

She was already at work when he got there.

Alex said, "Hey, you started without me."

"I wasn't sure when you'd get back," Elise said curtly. "So, how was lunch?"

Alex couldn't hide his grin. "You're just not going to believe this. She propositioned me."

Elise's head jerked up. "She what?"

"She wants me to model for her. She's an artist, you know."

Elise began to laugh, softly at first, then building to a full roar before Alex finally broke in and said, "Hey, it's not that funny."

"Alex, you know how much I think of you, but modeling? Please."

He shrugged. "Yeah, that was my reaction, too. I'm saying no."

Elise shook her head. "No, you should do it. Just think, you don't want to give up the chance to be in one of her paintings."

Alex grabbed a load of sheets from the dryer. "Believe it or not, I'll learn to live without that particular honor."

As Elise continued folding sheets, she said, "I am sorry, I shouldn't have laughed. So what's new in Elkton Falls?"

"You heard that Oxford Hitchcock disappeared, didn't you?"

Elise shook her head. "You can't be serious. What happened to him?"

"Nobody knows. Sheriff Armstrong's looking into it."

Elise stacked a few sheets in the basket, then said, "I wonder if the sheriff's found anything out about Toby Sturbridge. Emma is beside herself with worry."

Alex said, "I don't blame her. It can't feel good, being one of the prime suspects in a murder case."

Elise paused a moment, then said, "She thinks the sheriff is convinced of her guilt. It is truly odd that Toby showed up in Elkton Falls on the day Emma and Mor get engaged."

Alex said, "I wonder how long he was in town. Emma said he'd been hounding her for money, but she didn't say how long it had been going on. I can't help wondering if there's anything else she's not telling us."

"Alex Winston, she's our friend. Emma could never have had anything to do with Toby's death."

Alex said, "I didn't say she was responsible, just that she might not have come completely clean with us. Besides, she's not the only one I'm worried about."

Elise put another sheet in the basket. "I've been wondering about Mor myself. No, it's impossible."

Alex shook off the talk. "I'm sure they're both innocent," he said. "That's why it's so important for us to prove Mor and Emma had nothing to do with it." Alex finished folding the last sheet, then said, "On a brighter note, Mor and I are lighting the beacon tonight, and I want you to see it from the top with us."

For a moment, Elise's face lit up with the joy of a six-year-old. "How in the world did you ever manage that? I thought you had to get written approval from the Town Council."

Alex grinned. "The switch is broken, so Mor's coming

out tonight to replace it and check the light. He's clearing it with Grady Hatch as a part of the allowed maintenance."

"I can't wait," Elise said as they finished their folding.

"Neither can I," Alex replied.

They were carrying the sheets back to the linen closet when Alex and Elise found the newlyweds waiting on them at the front desk.

"There you are. We thought you'd disappeared," Sheila said.

Paul said, "Patience is a virtue, my dear."

"So is having a spine," she said, then turned to Alex. "We'd like a tour of the inn."

Elise said, "I'll go ahead and put these away," as she walked past them.

Great, now he was stuck with the battling honeymooners. "Well, I'd be glad to show you the grounds. There's the lighthouse itself, it's open during daylight hours only. Then there are Bear Rocks, they are really worth a visit. We've got a pond just down the road, and canoes are available for a slight additional fee."

Sheila said, "That's all just fine, but what we're really interested in are the guestrooms themselves."

Alex shook his head. "Sorry, those are off-limits. We respect everyone's privacy here," he added pointedly.

Paul stepped in. "Of course, we understand completely. I should have explained earlier, my bride and I are real lighthouse fanatics. Actually, we're as interested in the two keepers' quarters you have here as much as we are in the tower itself. Your place really caught our attention, and we'd love the complete tour." He was trying to shake Alex's hand again for some odd reason. Then Alex spotted the folded bill in his hand.

At that moment, Mrs. Nesbitt came downstairs. Alex said, "You really should speak with our visiting historian. Mrs. Nesbitt, do you have a moment?"

"Absolutely, Alex. What can I do for you?"

Alex said, "Mrs. Nesbitt, I'd like you to meet Paul and Sheila Jones. They've come to the inn on their honeymoon, and they're lighthouse enthusiasts as well."

Mrs. Nesbitt's face lit up. "Oh, that's simply outstanding. We must talk," she said as she took a hand of each of them.

"Well, we're really not all *that* well versed," Sheila said, trying to extricate her hand.

"Then I'd be delighted to educate you, my dear. My great-great-grandfather was an assistant keeper at the Body Island Lighthouse on the Outer Banks, you know."

"Really," Sheila said blandly.

If Mrs. Nesbitt caught her lukewarm tone, she didn't let on. "Why don't we climb to the top of the tower and I'll tell you about him. Old Jerab was a crusty fellow, let me tell you."

As they were led away to the lighthouse, Alex fought to hide his smile. It looked as though the newlyweds were going to get a thorough tour after all. And the best thing was, he didn't have to lead it.

Alex spotted them again over an hour later coming out of the lighthouse itself, heading for the utility shed next to it, no doubt to be regaled with more of Great-great-grandfather Jerab's adventures. Though the couple continued to try to break away, Mrs. Nesbitt was in no hurry to rid herself of her new charges until she'd imparted every ounce of her lighthouse lore to them.

6

Alex was happy to see Mor drive up in his truck as dusk approached Hatteras West.

After the handyman got out, Alex said, "I bet it feels good to get your truck back."

Mor slapped the hood. "Yeah, Irene said it was clean. She even had the boys run it through the car wash after they were finished with it. They did a good job, inside and out."

"Have you had any problem riding around in it after what happened?" Alex asked.

Mor said, "It was kind of creepy at first, but after half an hour I kind of forgot all about it. Life goes on, you know?"

"It does indeed. So where's Emma? I figured she'd be coming out with you."

Mor put on his tool belt more out of habit than need as he explained, "She was right behind me, so she should be here any minute. Is Elise coming, too?"

Alex said, "She wouldn't miss it for the world."

Mor grinned. "Then let's get to it."

They walked up the steel steps in single file, Mor's tool

belt clanking a little each time as he moved. When they got to the top landing, the handyman said, "Now let me take a look at this."

Mor killed the circuit breaker tucked over by the door going up to the lens itself, then unscrewed the switch and hooked it up to a meter secured onto his belt.

"Is that the problem?" Alex asked.

Mor studied the readings for a second, handed the old switch to Alex, then said, "It's deader than a doornail." Alex had dreaded changing the button to a modern switch, so he was delighted when Mor pulled a replica out of his shirt pocket.

Alex asked, "Where'd you find that?"

"You know Les, he subscribes to every magazine he can find, and his name must be on a list for all the catalogue folks, too. A couple of months ago I spotted one that handled old-house reproductions. I knew this thing would wear out sooner or later, so I wanted to be ready when you needed it."

Alex slapped the big man's shoulder. "Thanks, I really appreciate that. That's one bill I'll be glad to pay."

Mor shrugged. "Hey, you've done your best to keep us in business. This one's on the house."

After making up the new connections, Mor screwed the plate back in place and flipped the breaker. "You ready to try it?" he asked Alex.

"Without Elise and Emma? They'd both have my hide. No thanks."

"So let's go take in the view while we wait on them," Mor said.

The two men walked out onto the observation platform and leaned on the outer rail, taking in the growing twilight and the fresh breeze of the night air.

There was an easy, comfortable silence between them that was broken only by a police siren echoing in the distance.

Mor shook his head. "It sounds like old Strong Arms is on another bad guy's trail."

"He does like his light and siren. Has he said anything else to you about Sturbridge?"

Mor shook his head. "Truth be told, I've been doing my best to avoid him, and he hasn't come looking for me."

Alex said, "I guess that's a good sign."

From below, Alex saw Elise come out onto the porch and wave to them. She had a picnic basket tucked under one arm, and a blanket draped across her shoulders. From the other direction up Point Road, they saw Emma driving toward them.

Mor said, "Looks like the party's about to get started."

"I'm ready."

As the two women disappeared together into the base of the lighthouse, Mor said, "So the big day's finally here."

Alex asked, "Changing the switch? It's not that big a deal."

Mor said, "I'm talking about your date with Elise. It's about time, if you ask me."

Alex smiled. "If you ask me, it's past time. Tomorrow night's been a long time coming."

"Are you taking her to Charlotte for some fancy dinner?"

Alex said, "No, we can't afford the time away, not with an inn full of guests."

Mor said, "I hope you're at least going to Hickory. They've got some pretty nice places there."

Alex answered, "We're going to Mama Ravolini's. It's the best I could manage with the time we've got. Irma's promised me the best table in the house, though."

Mor shook his head. "Alex my friend, after all these years studying at my feet, I thought you'd be able to come up with something better than that for your first date with Elise."

Alex laughed. "You must not be half the teacher you thought you were."

Mor pretended to consider that for a moment, then said, "No, even a brilliant teacher can't do anything with a backward student."

Alex couldn't help the laugh that escaped just as the ladies joined them.

"What's so funny?" Elise asked.

Mor said, "Just some man talk."

Emma smiled briefly. "Discussing curtains and manicures again, boys?"

Mor said, "Enough guff, woman." He gestured to Elise. "What's in that basket?"

"I made some baloney sandwiches and brought some warm milk. I thought a picnic snack might be fun," she said, though it was apparent to all from the delightful aroma emanating from the basket that she'd fried chicken for their impromptu picnic dinner.

"That's too bad," Mor said. "What I really had a hankering for was some fried chicken."

Alex said, "Should we eat first or go ahead and light the beacon?" He was getting those butterflies again, eager to light the lens. The air was charged with electricity; it was almost as if the lighthouse itself sensed what was coming, and Alex fed off it.

Emma said, "Why don't we eat first? That way we can enjoy the light without worrying about attracting every moth in seven counties."

Mor put an arm around her. "That's why I love this woman. She's so practical."

Emma rolled her eyes. "And that's why I love you, you big moose. I just adore the way you sweet-talk me."

Elise laughed as she started to spread the blanket out on the platform. Alex grabbed the other end and they soon had it down, though the tug of the wind threatened to displace it. Mor said, "I can take care of that," and promptly sat down in the middle of everything.

"That's fine, but now there's no room for the rest of us," Emma said.

He moved over, and the four of them anchored their respective corners. Elise made a show of peeking inside the basket, then said, "Shoot."

"Forget something?" Alex asked. "I'll be glad to go back down for it."

Elise said, "No, it's too late for that. I meant to put a baloney sandwich in here to tease Mor with, but I must have left it on the counter."

Emma said, "Knowing him, he found it and already ate it."

Elise passed out plates, cups, and silverware, then started pulling food out of the hamper at a surprising rate.

Mor asked, "Any sweet tea in there?" as he reached for a peek into the basket.

Emma slapped his hand. "You just wait and see, you choosy beggar."

Elise pulled out a container of tea. "I wouldn't forget that. Alex, would you mind pouring?"

Alex opened the jar of tea, poured a little into his cup, and treated it like a fine wine. "It's got a robust flavor with a hint of playfulness; an unpretentious little vintage."

"Give me that, you big goofball," Mor said as he swiped the tea.

After dining on fried chicken, potato salad, and home-made rolls, Mor said, "I don't suppose you have any pie in there, do you?"

Emma said, "Even if she did, where in the world would you put it?"

"Hey, I'm a growing boy. I need to eat to keep my strength up."

She patted his stomach. "If you grow any more, you're going to have to buy new clothes."

Mor said indignantly, "I'll have you know I'm the perfect weight for my height."

Alex said, "I need to see that chart," as he helped Elise clean up. "Is everybody ready for the lighting?"

"Absolutely," Mor said. "Why don't you two go fire it up? Emma and I will watch it from here."

Alex said, "Don't forget, face outward. That lens puts out some real light."

"We'll be careful," Emma said. Though they had enjoyed a good meal with fine fellowship, Alex had noted a reserve in Emma that wouldn't go away. It was obvious that Toby Sturbridge's death was on all their minds, a real presence at their picnic, though no one brought up the man's death.

It was the best way to deal with it, at least until they had more information.

Alex and Elise walked inside to the switch, and Alex said, "Will you do the honors?"

"Are you serious? I know how much you love doing it, Alex. You go ahead."

Alex said, "Please, Elise, I'd like you to. The last time I lit it, you weren't around to see it."

Elise nodded. "I'm so sorry I missed the last Lighting. Alex, are you sure?"

"Absolutely."

With a schoolgirl's grin, Elise said, "I'd love to."

She punched the switch, and the light above them jumped to life. After a moment, it started to turn on its base. They walked out to the platform and watched as the beam cut through the countryside, leaving a path of light wherever it touched. There was sudden cheering from down below, and Alex saw several of his guests on the porches of the two buildings looking up at them. The beam ran through three circuits before Mor said, "You know the rules, Alex, three times around and it's got to go off. Grady was pretty clear about that today."

He nodded. "Elise, do you want to cut it off?"

"I can't hog all the fun. You go ahead."

Alex walked back inside to the switch, his finger hovering over it just a second before he finally killed the light.

Things went suddenly dark without the light, and Alex stood there until his eyes grew accustomed to the night. The cheers below had heartened him. Many of his guests came to the inn to see the lighthouse working, and nearly all of them were disappointed when they discovered that the light was usually dark. Blast it all, he needed to get the Town Council to let him light it more. He could position the lens toward the mountains where not many folks lived and leave it on for just a minute or two every night before it swung back on Elkton Falls. If Tracy was elected mayor, he was going to enlist her support and make it happen.

Maybe then they could keep the inn as full as it was at the moment, and Alex would have a chance to actually make a decent profit.

Elise and Emma led the way down the stairs with sturdy flashlights Alex had brought up. By the time they got to the base, the guests had already gone back inside.

Mor said, "Well, that was worth the cost of admission, no doubt about it." He turned to Emma. "Are you ready to head back into town?"

"I'm ready," she said as they all offered their good nights.

Mor said, "I'll follow you back. I don't want you getting into any trouble."

"Then who's going to watch you?" she asked with a smile.

Soon enough, it was just Alex and Elise.

"I'll help you wash the dishes," Alex said.

She stifled a yawn. "Actually, I'm beat. I think I'll do them in the morning."

That was odd. Usually they lingered over shared tasks in the evening, enjoying each other's company. There was no doubt about it. Something, however subtle, was changing between them.

Alex was still pondering the mood shift when Paul and Sheila, the newlyweds, rushed in. "You lit up the lighthouse," Sheila said in disgust.

"We had to replace a switch, so we did a check of the light."

She snapped, "You don't have to tell me, we heard about it in town. Paul and I were eating in some dreadful place called Mama Ravioli's or some such nonsense when someone rushed in to announce it. By the time we got outside, the light was off. I demand you turn it on again."

Alex said, "Sorry, I wish I could, but there's a town ordinance that says I can't. This was a special case."

Paul reached for his wallet and said, "Surely another

minute or two won't hurt. She's really got her heart set on it."

Alex declined. "I do apologize, I should have said something."

Jan and Corki came downstairs and spotted Alex talking with the newlyweds.

Jan said, "Oh, Alex, that was wonderful."

Corki added, "Absolutely spectacular. I can't believe we actually got to see it."

Jan said, "I got pictures!"

As the two ladies walked past toward the door, the newlyweds turned and headed upstairs without another word.

From the look of things, it was going to be another night of marital unbliss for them.

Alex had just finished his nightly rounds of checking both buildings and locking the lighthouse up when he heard a car approaching on the gravel drive.

He was startled to see Sheriff Armstrong getting out of his patrol car. Had he found something so urgent he needed to talk to Alex this late?

There was a grim look on his face as he got out of his squad car.

"What's going on?" Alex asked.

"It's Oxford Hitchcock."

"What about him?" Alex asked as his heart went cold.

Armstrong took a deep breath, let it out slowly, then said, "It's bad news, Alex. He's dead."

7

Alex asked, "I don't suppose there's any chance he died of natural causes, is there?"

Armstrong shook his head. "No, there's no doubt about it. Somebody walloped him upside the head with a board. It looks like they snuck up on him and hit him from behind."

Alex took it all in, then asked quietly, "Where was he, at his house?"

"That's the oddest part of all. We found Oxford hanging under the old covered bridge. He fell through one of those big holes your committee is trying to patch up. Anyway, his suspenders caught on one of the braces below, else he would have drifted down the river toward Charlotte by now. A couple of teenagers were down by the river making out and the guy flashed his light up under the bridge. We had the devil of a time getting the body down."

Elise came out into the lobby, dressed in a thick robe. "What's going on? Is it something about Mor or Emma?"

Alex said, "No, it's something else entirely. You can go back to bed if you'd like."

Ignoring him, Elise said, "What happened, Sheriff?"

"Somebody killed Oxford Hitchcock at the old covered bridge," the sheriff answered calmly.

Elise shook her head in disbelief. "Why would anyone do such a thing?"

Armstrong said, "That's what I'm aiming to find out. Alex, do you have any idea where Tracy Shook is?"

"Sheriff, you can't seriously consider her a suspect. I've known Tracy all my life. I can't see her doing something like this."

Armstrong rubbed his scalp. "Alex, every murderer in the history of the world knew somebody, and the fact is, just about every one of them had friends. People do things for the craziest reasons."

Alex couldn't believe the sheriff was serious. "You actually believe she'd kill him to get a job that pays nine thousand dollars a year? You're way off on this one."

Armstrong took off his hat, then rubbed a hand through his hair. "Alex, I didn't come out here for crime-fighting tips, I'm looking for Tracy. Once I talk to her, maybe we can clear her right off the bat, but you can bet your last hat I'm going to talk to her tonight."

"Sorry, I haven't seen her," Alex said.

Armstrong looked at Elise. "And you, Ma'am?"

"No, I'm sorry I can't help."

Armstrong nodded briefly, then put his hat back on. "If she comes out here, call me. I don't care what time of day or night."

"I still say she didn't do it," Alex insisted.

Armstrong just smiled. "You're forgetting one thing, Alex."

"What's that?"

The sheriff said, "You don't get a vote."

After the sheriff was gone, Elise said, "I can't imagine anyone killing that nice man, and I certainly can't see Tracy doing it."

"The sheriff's way off on this one." He stretched, then added, "I can't see getting to sleep any time soon. Care to join me for a hot chocolate?"

She stifled a yawn. "Thanks for the offer, but I'm going back to bed."

"Good night, then," he said.

Later, Alex went to sleep wondering who had cause enough to kill Oxford Hitchcock. To Alex, he was just a typical politician, but to someone, the man must have been a real threat.

At least Alex wasn't involved in that particular investigation. He had enough on his hands trying to get Mor and Emma off the sheriff's list of prime suspects for Toby Sturbridge's death.

Alex opened the newspaper the next day to see if there were any new details about Elkton Falls' latest murder. The headline announcing the murder took up half the page, accompanied by a head shot of the victim and tons of background, but it didn't offer anything he didn't already know. Alex wondered briefly if Armstrong had ever found Tracy, but then put it out of his mind as Elise walked in.

"Morning," he said as he offered her the paper. "How'd you sleep?"

"I tossed and turned all night," she said.

"Yeah, I'm pretty excited, too," Alex admitted.

"About that man's death? Alex, that's not like you."

Alex said, "I'm talking about our date. It's tonight, remember?"

Elise said, "Of course I do." She finished the breakfast setup without another word about it. He wanted to say something else to her, but before he had a chance, Corki and Jan came down, followed by Denise and Greg, a couple who were rockhounds on their way to Hiddenite, and on their heels came Paul and Sheila, the battling newlyweds. The lobby of the inn was buzzing with conversation, but nothing substantial was spoken between Alex and Elise.

The housekeeper finally said, "If you don't mind, I'm going to go ahead and get an early start on Dual."

"That's fine, I can take care of things here." He took a

deep breath, then added, "Listen, if you don't want to go out tonight, that's okay with me."

Elise's lips were pressed together in a thin white line. "No, tonight will be fine."

Alex laughed in spite of himself. "It will be a lot better than fine, I can promise you that."

Elise smiled softly. "Of course it will. I'll see you later."

"Bye," he said as she hurried away. Elise had something on her mind, and Alex thought for a moment he should go ahead and cancel their date. But he just couldn't bring himself to do it. They had both waited too long for this, and he doubted he could stand another delay.

As Alex waited for the guests to finish their breakfasts so he could clean up, he took a chance and dialed Doc Drake at his office. Madge, the doctor's nurse who also happened to be his wife, answered the phone.

"Hi, Madge. Any chance I can steal a minute from your husband?"

Madge said with a snort, "You're welcome to try your luck talking to him. I'm surely not having any luck."

Drake came on the phone, and Alex asked, "Trouble in paradise?"

The doctor said, "You don't even want to know. Madge has been after me to take a vacation, but I don't know how we can get away."

"Hey, you still owe her a honeymoon," Alex said. "We'll manage to limp along without you somehow."

Drake spoke to his wife and said, "Alex thinks you're being unreasonable, too."

He could hear Madge's laughter through the line. "I know better than that. He's backing me up, isn't he?"

Drake admitted, "Yes, but what does he know? He's still a bachelor."

Alex said, "Much as I'd like to be your couples therapist, I was wondering if you've had any luck with Toby Sturbridge."

"Well, at this point, all I can say for sure is that I'm pretty certain he's still dead."

"No clues at all?"

Drake said, "I'm out of my league on this one. I've got a special coroner coming from Raleigh, but he won't be here for three days."

"Three days? What's the delay?"

Drake mumbled something into the phone Alex couldn't hear.

"Repeat that, Doc, I missed it."

Drake took a deep breath, then said loudly, "He's on vacation in Hawaii."

Madge's whoop of laughter in the background was more than the doctor could take. "I've got to go, Alex. I'll let you know when I find something else out."

Without an official cause of death, the sheriff would probably back off from the case until he had a definite idea about what had really happened to Toby Sturbridge. Besides, he had his hands full with Oxford Hitchcock's murder. Alex admired Doc Drake as much for his abilities as for knowing his limitations. A thorough job was important, and if they had to wait, then there was no escaping it.

Alex had just finished cleaning the newlyweds' room when he heard someone call him from the hallway. As he stepped out with his cart, he saw Tracy Shook standing in front of the main desk.

"I'm over here," he called out, emptying the trash can topped off with *The Tattle Tale*, a weekly supermarket gossip sheet that favored alien babies and Elvis sightings, into his cart's bin. He never would have pegged the newlyweds, with their "his" and "hers" matching notebook computers as readers of the rag, but then that was one of the most interesting things about being an innkeeper: folks were constantly surprising him. From the rumpled blankets and pillow in the corner, it looked as if Mr. Jones had spent last night on the floor again. If the way the two of them argued was any indication, Alex wondered if the man ever got to actually sleep in the bed.

Tracy said, "Alex, I just had to come by and talk to you. Have you heard the news?"

"Armstrong told us last night. I'm sorry about Oxford. I know he was a friend of yours."

Tracy said, "I'm sorry too, for more reasons than you can imagine. That's not what I'm talking about, though. I won't even make you guess. This is all so insane. Conner's decided to take Oxford's place and run against me. He's already got his campaign slogan: 'Vote for the Right Shook'. Can you believe that?"

Alex said, "I hate to say it, but it sounds exactly like something Conner would do. Did Armstrong find you last night?"

She nodded. "He tracked me down at Mama Ravolini's. The first quiet meal I've had since I started this campaign, and the sheriff joins me for a late dinner to interrogate me. He even asked me for an alibi, if you can imagine that."

"I told him you couldn't have done it. Was he satisfied with your whereabouts?"

Tracy said, "Not particularly. I was home alone most of the afternoon when I wasn't out searching for Oxford. I had the phone off the hook so I could get some peace and quiet, and nobody came to my door, so I guess I don't have any alibi at all. I didn't kill him, Alex. We were opponents, but I genuinely liked the man."

"Don't worry, Armstrong will find the real killer."

"I hope so. I can't imagine what Conner will do with all of this."

Alex said, "Tracy, you can take the gloves off now and get a few shots in yourself. You know Conner's weaknesses better than anyone else in the world."

A mischievous grin crossed her face. "You know what? This might be fun after all. He's been hiding behind Oxford sniping at me. Now let's see how he likes it out on the front lines."

"There's the spirit," Alex said, glad to see the fire in his friend's eyes.

"I'm not letting him get away with this 'Right Shook' business either. I'll show him who the right Shook is. Alex, thanks for the pep talk."

"Hey, what are friends for? Is Shantara still helping you with your campaign?"

"Oh yes. That's where I'm going right now. With all of her customers, we've got a built-in support system." Shantara Robinson ran Elkton Falls' general store/craft gallery/mercantile. Tracy had chosen well. Not only was Shantara well liked by the community, but she had nearly as many visitors every day as Buck's Grill. Alex knew Buck had backed Oxford Hitchcock, but he wondered if there was a possibility that the big man would swing his support to Tracy instead of Conner.

Alex asked, "Have you thought about talking to Buck about supporting you now that Oxford's gone?"

"I tried, but he's backing Conner. I understand, he supports his party." Tracy smiled as she added, "Sally Anne's pulling for me though, so I've got a spy in the enemy camp."

With her dual assignments, Alex wondered when Sally Anne had time to wait on her customers.

Tracy said, "I've got to run, Alex. Thanks again for all your support."

"Let me know if there's anything I can do. I mean it."

She patted his cheek. "I know it. Bye now."

Alex finished his cleaning chores for the morning and was just about to look for Elise to offer her lunch when Mor drove up. Alex walked out and met him on the front porch. The big man was carrying two paper bags, a large one and a much smaller one.

"I didn't call you," Alex said with a grin.

"I know. I got lonely, with Les gone and all. You can't tell me nothing in this place is broken."

"Sorry, we're in good shape, but if you hang around long enough, I'm sure something will need fixing. What's in the bags?"

"A surprise, and lunch. I grabbed a couple of burgers at Buck's. You supply the Cokes and we'll eat out here."

Alex said, "You feeling okay?"

"Yeah, I'm fine," Mor said, puzzled. "Why do you ask?"

"The last time you bought me a meal, I was in the ninth grade and Greg Frye had just stolen my lunch money."

Mor shrugged. "I need to talk to you about some wedding stuff, so I thought we'd do it over burgers."

Alex grabbed two Cokes and met Mor back out on the porch. Mor said, "I got a hamburger for Elise, too."

"I don't know where she disappeared to. I guess I'll just have to eat it myself," Alex added with a grin.

"Tell you what, we'll arm-wrestle for it."

"Why don't you go ahead? I'd hate to deprive you."

After taking a few bites, Alex asked, "So what do we need to talk about for the wedding?"

Mor looked down at his feet. "It's not exactly the wedding. It's more like the bachelor party."

Alex laughed. "Don't worry, I know how to throw you a party."

Mor said, "That's just it. Emma's putting her foot down. No women, no carrying on, shoot, I had to fight her to get alcohol approved. Beer's the best we can do."

"Is this a wake or a bachelor party? I can't imagine the most eligible bachelor in seven counties giving up his last rite without a fight."

"Well, you can believe it," Mor said. "We're both getting a little long in the tooth for that foolishness anyway. You know what I'd like, just between the two of us?"

"I don't have a clue," Alex said honestly.

"I'd like to grab a few beers with you and Les, toast the old life, then get to bed early. I've been to too many parties where the groom got so carried away he was barely awake to enjoy the ceremony the next day. No sir, my wild days are far behind me. Are you disappointed in me?" Mor asked, his gaze on the smaller bag in his hands.

"Are you kidding?" Alex asked. "I was almost looking forward to my speech compared to throwing you a bachelor party."

Mor said, "That's a relief. So it's settled. It's going to be just three old bachelors hanging out and trading stories one last night."

"Sounds like a plan to me," Alex agreed. "Okay, if you're not going to bring it up, I will. What's in the other bag?"

Mor held it out to him. "Reach in and see."

Alex put his hand in the bag gingerly and pulled out a small square of wood with an *E* etched on its face. He dug his hand back in and found ten more *E*'s inside, all carefully lettered and smoothly polished.

Mor said, "I know the inn's Scrabble game lost all of its *E*'s when one of your guests took them as souvenirs, so I decided to make you some new ones."

"The game won't be as challenging this way," Alex admitted with a smile. "Thanks, I appreciate this."

Mor said, "Hey, it's the least I can do for someone who's not going to throw me a bachelor party."

Alex laughed. "I can do better than that. I won't throw you a birthday party either when March 11 rolls around."

Mor looked at his watch, then said, "I'd better get moving. I've got a list of jobs a mile long to do at Grady Hatch's place. Did you hear he's putting his house up for sale? He wants to buy a motor home and see the world. I've got to admit, there's a part of me that would love to go with him."

"You'd get bored in three days, and we both know it. You've got to have something to do to keep yourself busy, my friend, and your roots go down in this soil as deeply as mine do."

Mor grinned. "It's true enough, but a man can dream, can't he?"

"They haven't found a way to tax it yet," Alex agreed as Mor left.

Alex half expected to find Elise working in the lobby, but she was nowhere to be found. The butterflies were in full force now.

Their date was only a few hours away.

8

Alex felt like a teenager waiting for Elise in the lobby of
the Main Keeper's Quarters. He had on his best suit, actually his only suit, since there wasn't much need to wear
one in his line of work. His truck, as old as it was, was
freshly washed, and he held three roses he'd gotten in town
for Elise.

Paul Jones, the newlywed, came out while Alex was
waiting for Elise. "Have you seen Sheila?" he asked, taking in Alex's attire.

"No, sorry, I haven't."

Paul gestured to the flowers. "Okay, I'll bite. What have
you got, a big date?"

Alex nodded. "The biggest."

Paul shook his head and laid a hand on Alex's shoulder.
"Be careful, my friend. That's all I'm going to say."

"Thanks for the advice," Alex said, fighting to hide his
smile.

Enough of this waiting around, Alex thought to himself.
He knocked on Elise's door, the flowers nearly strangled in
his nervous grip.

Elise had on a sundress, nothing fancy or formal by any

stretch of the imagination, but she looked absolutely stunning to him.

He offered her the flowers. "Here. These are for you."

She didn't take them at first. "Alex, I didn't realize this was going to be so formal. Give me a few minutes and I'll change."

"You look great just the way you are," he said as he held the roses out again.

She took the flowers, then said, "Nonsense. I can be ready in ten minutes."

"Elise, it isn't necessary. You really do look great."

She shoved him gently back toward the lobby. "But we don't match."

Alex protested, "Then let me change."

Elise wouldn't hear of it. "Go on, I won't be long."

There was no nonsense in her voice, and Alex knew this was a battle he wasn't about to win. Should he have told her they were dressing up for dinner? Granted, Mama Ravolini's wasn't exactly the Ritz, but it was the best Elkton Falls had to offer for fine dining. He often wondered why no other restaurateur tackled Elkton Falls. Though he loved the owner Irma Bean dearly, a little variety in eating dinner out would have been nice.

Elise was as good as her word, coming out ten minutes later wearing a fancy shimmering blue dress that barely touched her knees. She'd swept back part of her hair, too, adding a formal touch, instead of the casual ponytail she usually wore during working hours.

Alex said, "Wow. You look wonderful."

"Thanks. And thanks for the flowers. You shouldn't have."

"I couldn't help myself," Alex admitted as he grinned. "Let's go."

He had placed a sign on the front desk that said, OUT FOR THE EVENING, and Elise asked, "Are you sure about deserting our guests like this?"

"They'll be fine without us for one night," Alex said.

He held her door open as she slid onto the truck seat.

She really was stunning. Alex couldn't believe they were finally going out on a real date.

Oddly enough, their conversation, normally as free flowing as a river, was dammed into a few uncomfortable remarks on their way into town. A new tension had sprung up between them, and as hard as he tried, Alex just couldn't seem to break the strain.

"Is everything all right?" he finally asked as they neared the restaurant.

"It's fine," Elise said.

Alex said, "You know, my mom used to say everything was fine when what she meant was that it was simply bearable. That's not the case here, is it?"

Elise said, "Alex, when I say something's fine, it's fine. Don't read anything into it."

"Sorry, my mistake," he replied as he slid into a parking spot.

Elise, realizing her words had been too sharp, said, "I guess this is just new to me, being out with you like this."

"We spend all day together every day," he said.

"Not like this."

Alex opened her door. "No, you're right. This is better."

Irma made a fuss over them as they walked in the door, leading Alex and Elise to a table with a RESERVED placard on it. "You two look wonderful. Now enjoy yourselves."

As the first course arrived, Alex said, "I took the liberty of ordering your favorites ahead of time."

Elise just nodded.

Alex found himself fiddling with his napkin, searching for something to say that had nothing to do with the Hatteras West Inn or their guests. Surely the two of them had more in common than their work. So why was it suddenly so hard to think of anything?

As a desperate last measure, he said, "You'll never believe this, but I found a marked-up copy of *The Tattle Tale* in the newlyweds' room."

"No work talk, remember," Elise said. They had agreed on that beforehand.

"Sorry. So what's new with you?" he asked.

"Nothing since we spoke this afternoon," Elise admitted.

Somehow they got through dinner, but Alex found that he was relieved to be driving back to Hatteras West. Something had gone terribly wrong with the evening, and he didn't have a clue how it had happened. All his expectations, all his preparations, and they had ended up having a terrible time.

He couldn't just let it die, not like that. Instead of driving directly back to the inn, Alex stopped at Bear Rocks.

Elise asked, "What's wrong?"

Alex grinned. "Well, I figured we should go ahead and get our 'good night' kiss out of the way before we get back to the inn." Before Elise could say anything, Alex added, "Relax, I'm just kidding. Man, that was one huge disaster, wasn't it?"

Elise said in a near-whisper, "Alex, I'm so sorry. It's all my fault."

Alex replied, "I'm not about to let you take all the credit. Let's make a list of my mistakes tonight. I was way overdressed for Irma's, the flowers were probably over the top, I shouldn't have ordered our food ahead of time without at least asking you. Let's see, did I leave anything out?"

Elise laughed, a sound that was sheer joy to his ears. "I think you were sweet. We both put too much pressure on ourselves to possibly have a good time. It was dreadful, wasn't it?"

Alex joined her laughter. "It was indeed pretty painful. So does this mean we've passed permanently into the 'friends' zone?"

"I don't know," Elise admitted.

"I, for one, hope not," Alex said, keeping his gaze locked forward. "Elise, the more I get to know you, the more I care for you. You've become a good friend, but I've got to admit, every time I see you, my heart jumps a little. I just wish this would have worked out."

"Me, too. Believe me, Alex. So what do we do now?"

Alex admitted, "I'm at a complete loss. I was hoping you'd know."

Elise nodded. "I don't. We might as well go back to the inn."

"I guess you're right. Sorry our evening was such a bust."

She hesitated a moment, then said, "I am, too. Let's just put this behind us."

He nodded. "I guess that's the only thing we can do."

Alex drove back to the inn, walked her to her door, then said, "Good night, Elise."

She leaned forward and kissed him gently on the lips, a peck so brief he could barely believe it had happened. "Don't give up yet, Alex. My heart's been known to skip when you're around, too. Nobody said this was going to be easy."

"Nothing worthwhile usually is," he said as she disappeared into her room.

Alex was left with nothing but the gentle reminder of her perfume in the air, and the memory of the slight pressure of her presence near him.

For tonight, it would have to be enough.

The next day, things were still a little awkward between them, and Alex wondered if that particular dream of them ever being together was dead beyond all hope. Truth be told, after breakfast he was happy enough to go off on his own cleaning Main while she tackled Dual.

He was just finishing the hallway sweeping when he heard someone calling him from downstairs. Conner Shook was the last person on earth Alex expected to find visiting his inn.

"Alex, how are you?" There was no way to tell from the warm tone in his voice that the two of them had stopped talking since Conner's marriage with Tracy had broken up.

"Conner," Alex said evenly. "What can I do for you?"

"It's about this mayoral race. I was hoping to talk to you about throwing your support my way."

Alex could barely believe the man's gall. "Conner, you know better than that. Tracy and I have been friends forever."

"Friendship is one thing, but the office of mayor is something else altogether. Tell me something, Alex, do you really see Tracy running Elkton Falls?"

"I think she's just what this town needs," Alex said.

Conner shrugged. "Okay, that's fine, I understand, but if you change your mind, I'd be happy to have your support."

"I wouldn't count on it if I were you, Conner."

The man just laughed. "By the time the election rolls around, you might not have a choice."

"What are you implying?" Alex asked, the steel coming out in his voice.

Conner said, "The last I heard, Sheriff Armstrong was looking hard at Tracy as a suspect in Oxford's murder."

Alex said coldly, "How about you, Conner? Do you have an alibi for that night?"

"I was in Charlotte on business, not that it's any of your concern."

Alex wasn't about to let up. "That's mighty convenient, Conner. Is there any way you can prove you were there the entire time?"

"I don't have to," Conner said, the schoolyard bully coming out in his voice. "I'm not a suspect."

"At least not that you know of," Alex said.

"Why? What have you heard? I know you and Armstrong are tight. What did he say to you?"

"That he's still looking," Alex said. That much was true.

Conner's expression froze for a moment, then he forced a smile to his lips. "Alex, I've got nothing to hide. The sheriff can look all he wants to." Conner started to walk away, but he paused and called back, "Let me know if you change your mind."

"It's not happening, Conner."

He just shrugged. "Have a good day, then."

After he was gone, Alex stood there silently in thought, wondering about the real reason Conner Shook had come out to the inn. One thing was certain: he was lying about being there to solicit Alex's support. Conner knew too well that he supported Tracy.

So what was it, a fishing expedition? Could Conner have had anything to do with the murder of his candidate? He could have been after the limelight himself. Perhaps Oxford Hitchcock had gotten in the way of Conner's big plans to take over the campaign himself.

Alex was just finishing up his chores when he heard someone drive up in the parking lot. That was one of the great things about having a gravel drive; cars usually announced themselves well before the occupants arrived. This was certainly the inn's day for visitors.

Alex was happy to see Grady Hatch come in.

"Mayor, what brings you out here?"

Grady said sternly, "I got a handful of complaints about that overgrown night-light of yours out there, and I promised I'd follow up on them."

Alex stammered, "Mor said he cleared it with you beforehand."

Grady's hard expression melted away. "Relax Alex, I was just pulling your chain. Truth to tell, a couple of folks thought you should light it up every night."

"I've been meaning to talk to you about that. What are the odds the Town Council will loosen up their restrictions on it?"

"I'd say somewhere between slim and none. You want me to take another run at them, Alex? My term's almost up, but I wouldn't mind tumbling with that group one more time. I can tell you what the answer's going to be ahead of time, though. Alex, folks like you fine, but your big old flashlight in their living room is not something that makes them overly fond of you. It doesn't help matters that Madelyn Rose lives within eyeshot. She called me yesterday morning screaming her head off about you breaking the law. I finally got her calmed down when I told her you were doing regular maintenance, but she was still as mad as a wet cat when we got off the phone. Why don't you wine and dine her instead of that pretty maid of yours? Maybe she'd get off your back then."

Alex had been waiting for the first volleys to be fired about his date with Elise. It certainly hadn't taken the town of Elkton Falls long to pick up on the latest bit of gossip. He was just unhappy that there were no other fruits of the date than everyone else's idle speculation.

"I doubt I'd do much good with either one of them at this point," Alex admitted.

Grady slapped his back and laughed. "The ways of love are wild and unpredictable, my friend. You can't give up just when you're finally getting started."

Alex had heard just about all the advice he cared to hear. "I appreciate your concern, but I can't believe you'd drive all the way out here to talk to me about my love life and my lighthouse."

Grady said, "Well, I just felt like a drive, truth told. Say, what do you think about Oxford Hitchcock? Terrible thing, isn't it?"

"Were you two close?" Alex asked.

"No, we worked on a few projects together, but there was nothing personal between us. Still and all, he was a fine man, and he would have been good for Elkton Falls."

"How about Tracy?" Alex asked. "Please tell me you're not backing Conner."

Harry shook his head. "Alex my friend, I'm not endorsing anyone. Nope, I promised myself I'd stay out of this election, and that goes double when we've got exes battling it out." He winked at Alex as he added, "It should be a whale of a fight though, don't you think?"

Alex nodded. "I'm dreading the debate."

Grady slapped him on the back. "That's when I expect to see the most fireworks. I'm introducing them both next week at the debate, then I'm getting off the stage before they light into each other." He glanced at his watch as he added, "Well, sir, I've got to go. Oh, by the way, did you hear we postponed our 'Save the Bridge' meeting until after the election?"

"How's the fund-raising going?" Alex asked.

"Oh, slow but steady. Folks don't want to give much to the cause. I've been hitting up some of our local businesses, but so far it's just trickling in. Don't worry though, we'll see that old bridge repaired sooner or later, I promise you that."

"I didn't think you made campaign promises," Alex said, teasing.

"In this case, I'll make an exception. See you around, Alex."

An hour later Mor came in as Alex was putting his broom away, and from the look on the big man's face, something new had gone very desperately wrong.

9

"What is it?" Alex asked, dreading to hear the answer to his question.

"It's Emma. She just turned herself in for killing her ex-husband."

The broom in Alex's hand fell to the floor, sending a crashing echo through the lobby.

"I can't believe that."

Mor said, "*You* can't? How about me? I'm in shock."

Alex said, "Tell me what happened."

Mor walked over to one of the tables set up for backgammon, a game he and Alex often enjoyed playing together. Neither one of them was in any mood for games at the moment, though.

Mor pushed the game aside and said, "Last night we had a long, drawn-out discussion about this whole thing, mostly about Toby just popping up like he did. Well, I got mad at her for not telling me about it when he first came to town." Mor looked at his hands folded in front of him, then added meekly, "I lost my temper and stormed out. Turns out she knew the guy was going to come around before he even stepped foot in Elkton Falls; she just didn't know when. You know me, I have a tendency to fly off the handle when it comes to Emma. The next thing I know, Sandra's calling me this morning and telling me Emma's in jail."

"I still can't believe it," Alex said.

"You've got to do something, Alex. I know she couldn't have killed him. I don't have any proof, but it's clear in my heart that she's innocent."

Alex studied the big man before speaking. He hated seeing his friend in such torment. "I want to help, but what can I do, Mor?"

"Talk to her. Convince her she's not helping anybody by pulling this stunt."

Alex said, "She'll listen to you better than she would to me, Mor."

The handyman shook his head, and Alex could see he was as close to tears as he'd been in ages. "That's just it. She won't see me."

Alex nodded. "I'll do what I can."

Mor struggled with his thanks, then hurriedly left the inn.

Alex went in search of Elise to tell her the news. As he hunted for the housekeeper, he couldn't help wondering if it was possible that Emma's confession was legitimate. He knew Toby Sturbridge had terrorized her during their marriage; Emma had confessed that much to him on several occasions. But could she have killed him? No, he wouldn't believe it if she told him herself.

Alex found Elise finishing up her rooms in Dual.

"I need a huge favor," Alex said.

Elise replied, "I've seen that look in your eyes before. You're going to meddle in this business with Oxford Hitchcock, aren't you?"

Alex shook his head. "Absolutely not, I'm staying clear of that one. Mor just came in and told me Emma's confessed to Toby Sturbridge's murder."

"That's ridiculous," Elise snapped.

"I think so too, but she's locked up over at the jail now, and she's refused to see Mor."

"Go talk to her, Alex. I can handle things here."

He smiled gently. "Thanks, Elise. I appreciate it."

"She's my friend too, Alex. Tell her I'll be by later to see her myself."

"Sheriff, you can't keep her locked away from everybody who cares about her," Alex said, fighting to keep his voice steady. He'd been battling Armstrong for ten minutes, trying to get the sheriff to allow him in to see Emma.

"Alex, I keep telling you, I can't do anything about it. She's made it pretty clear she doesn't want to see anybody. If you ask me, she's ashamed of what she did, and I can't say that I blame her. Murder's a bad business, no matter how nice the killer might be."

Alex asked, "How did she say she killed him? There wasn't a mark on him."

Armstrong stroked his chin. "She walked in first thing this morning and confessed. Emma said she did him in, and after that, I haven't heard another word out of her."

Alex said, "She didn't tell you because she doesn't know how he died."

"Alex, Emma's not the type to come in here and confess to something she didn't do. We get those crackpots now and then, but she's not one of them."

"I can't believe she could kill anybody. Now are you going to go ask her if she'll see me, or do I have to come back in ten minutes with Sandra?"

It was the threat of returning with the lawyer that finally worked; there was no doubt in Alex's mind about that.

"Okay, I'll ask, but we're both wasting our time. She's not going to talk to you."

Alex waited outside the detention area while Armstrong went to ask Emma. Looking out the window, he could see storm clouds building on the horizon. They were in the middle of a drought, and any rain would be welcome, but the blackness of the sky matched his mood. It was surreal, visiting one of his best friends in the Elkton Falls jail.

Armstrong came back rubbing his chin. "I guess you're

more special than I thought you were, Alex. She's agreed to see you."

As Alex started for the door, Armstrong said, "Listen, you're not her lawyer and these aren't regular visiting hours." Alex started to protest as Armstrong finished, "But I'm making an exception for you. I can give you five minutes, but that's it. Go on in the interrogation room and I'll bring her to you."

"Thanks, Sheriff," Alex said, glad for any time he could get with Emma.

Alex expected Emma Sturbridge to be wilted by the ordeal, so he was a little surprised to see her head held high as she came into the interrogation room.

Alex started to get up to hug her when Armstrong said, "No physical contact, Alex. I'm sorry, but those are the rules."

"I understand," Alex said. "Emma, how are you?"

She waited until the door closed, then said, "I'm fine, Alex. The sheriff's been truly nice. He even ran down to Shantara's and picked up a few magazines for me to read while I'm in here."

Alex took a deep breath, then said, "Do you mind telling me what this is all about?"

Emma shook her head. "Sorry, I'm not in the mood to talk."

"Then why did you agree to see me, blast it all," Alex said, letting some of his frustration seep through.

Emma smiled briefly, a flicker that was gone in a heartbeat. "I want you to tell Mor to stop trying to visit me. How is he, Alex?"

"He's fine, but then again, he's not the one who just confessed to murder."

Emma sighed. "I did what I had to do, Alex."

He said, "I can't believe you're in here."

"Oh, don't let that bother you another minute. It's not so bad."

Alex shook his head. "It's worse than you think. When you pulled this little stunt of yours, Armstrong stopped looking for the real killer."

Emma tipped her head to one side. "I didn't have any choice, Alex."

It suddenly hit him why she had put herself in that position. "You think Mor killed him, don't you?"

For the first time since she'd been ushered in, Emma broke eye contact with him.

Alex pushed on. "You confessed so Armstrong would quit hounding Mor. Admit it."

Emma, her gaze still on her hands, said, "Don't be foolish, Alex. I don't know what you're talking about."

"Emma Sturbridge, if you think I'm going to stand by and watch you throw yourself on your sword, you're out of your mind. Have some faith in Mor. He didn't kill Toby any more than you did."

Tears crept down her cheeks. "Alex, you didn't see him last night. He was so angry, about Toby and everything else."

"Emma, he wouldn't kill anybody, certainly not in his own truck. Even if Mor's temper got the better of him, don't you think he would have done something pretty obvious, like beating the man up? You saw Toby yourself. There wasn't a mark on him. They don't even have an official cause of death yet."

"Oh dear," Emma said, the enormity of what she'd done obviously sinking in at last. "Alex, I've made a dreadful mistake. How is Mor ever going to forgive me?"

Alex said, "Mor's the least of your problems. How are we going to get you out of here?"

"Never mind that. Call Mor. I've got to do something before it's too late."

Alex said, "I'm calling Sandra. After she gets you out, you can deal with Mor yourself."

"This is dreadful."

Alex took a chance on breaking Armstrong's rule and reached over to pat Emma's hand. "Sandra will straighten this out. In the meantime, don't say anything else. Okay?"

"I promise."

Armstrong tapped once on the door, then opened it. "Time's up. Sorry."

"We were just finished," Alex said.

"Make both those calls, Alex. Promise me," Emma said.

"As long as I can do it in the order I want to," Alex said with a slight grin.

"You're as stubborn as I am, Alex Winston."

"Talk to you soon, Emma."

After Armstrong took Emma back to her cell, he was surprised to find Alex on his telephone.

Alex hung up as the sheriff walked in. "That's for official business only, Alex."

"Sorry, I couldn't wait. Sheriff, you know as well as I do that confession's worthless."

Armstrong huffed, "Alex, don't go meddling in my business. You're just an innkeeper, remember?"

"I'm also Emma's friend."

Armstrong pointed to the telephone. "Who were you calling?"

"Sandra Beckett," Alex admitted. "She's on her way over here."

"Wonderful. That's just what I need."

Alex said, "Sorry. I know you didn't cause this yourself."

"I guess that's as much sympathy as I can hope for, isn't it? Now do me a favor and kindly get your carcass out of my office."

"I'm on my way," Alex said.

Alex knew Emma's confession had stirred up a hornet's nest. Sandra was a great attorney, but that didn't mean Emma would be sleeping in her own bed tonight. These things took time, and it was going to be hard to un-ring that particular bell. How matters would stand between Emma and Mor after she finally did get out was anyone's guess. One thing he was certain of: Mor wouldn't be thrilled that Emma had thought him capable of killing her ex-husband.

Alex knew in his heart that Emma's instincts were way off base. Mor himself could confess the crime on the news and Alex wouldn't believe it of his friend.

So if Mor hadn't killed the man, and Emma hadn't either, who or what exactly had ended Toby Sturbridge's life?

Since Alex was already in town, he decided to go by Shantara's General Store and see how things were going with Tracy Shook and her campaign against her ex-husband.

Shantara was with a customer in the craft section of her store, showing some of Bill Yadkin's blacksmith work to a sharp-eyed woman in an expensive suit.

The woman said, "Eleven hundred dollars for that piece? You've got to be kidding. You must be able to do better than that."

Shantara said, "No, Ma'am. This fellow's had offers all over the country for his work. He sells some of his creations here only as a favor to me because he's local."

When the woman saw that Shantara wasn't going to budge, she said, "Okay, you win. I'll take everything."

Shantara nodded as she began collecting a dozen forged hooks, a mirror with twining steel tendrils, and a gate with swirls of iron wrapped with black vines. Alex pretended to browse as he watched the register display light up. The total was staggering.

After the buyer made a trip to her car with her first load, Alex said, "Whew, I hope Bill appreciates your sales acumen."

Shantara laughed. "He does, but all I really need is the way my commission says thanks."

Alex said, "Come on, you were laying it on a little thick, weren't you? Bill Yadkin's good, but in demand all over the country?"

Shantara said, "Hey, it's true. A man came in the store from Foggy Bottom yesterday and bought a hook. If that's not out in the country, I don't know what is."

Their conversation was interrupted as the woman came back in. After gathering up the last of her purchases, she handed Shantara a business card. "Give this to the artisan, would you? I'd like to commission a matching piece for that sculpture."

Shantara said, "What exactly did you have in mind?"

"A complementary piece to the wall hanging, of course." It was all the woman could do to keep from rolling her eyes.

After she was gone, Shantara said, "And here I thought it was just a gate. Bill made it for Trinity Sloane, but when it came time to pay, the old coot stiffed him. I convinced Bill to let me sell it for him, but he swore up and down I was wasting my time."

"Hey, it looked like art to me," Alex said.

"So what brings you out here when you have an inn full of guests? I know you don't have time for social calls."

Alex said, "I'm worried about Tracy. How is the campaign going?"

Shantara said, "Oxford Hitchcock was bad enough, but running against Conner is turning out to be a real nightmare. Have you seen his latest stunt?"

When Alex said he hadn't, Shantara reached behind the counter and pulled out a poster. All it said was SHOOK in bold white letters with a green background.

"So? That's one of Tracy's, isn't it?"

Shantara said, "Don't I wish. No, we used red on our first run. He went to the same printer over in Hickory, used everything we did, but he changed the color. Folks around here are going to be voting for the Red Shook or the Green one."

"I don't see how it can help him, since it doesn't say which Shook to vote for."

"Alex, he's been telling everybody that Green means Go for Connor, and Red means stop Tracy from ruining Elkton Falls."

A sudden thought struck Alex. "Okay, here's a way to turn it around on him. Green also means untried and inexperienced. Use that against Conner."

Shantara smiled. "I knew there was a reason I kept you around. We'll do just that. Maybe we'll switch to a gold background for Tracy and throw his whole attack plan off."

Alex asked, "Whatever happened to the issues, or to a candidate's qualifications? Doesn't anybody even have a platform anymore?"

"Alex, they still do, but that's not what gets the voters excited. We're trying to come up with some flair to get their attention. Once they know we're out there, then they'll listen to what we stand for."

"If you say so," he said.

Shantara said, "Just leave it to me, Alex. I'll teach Conner Shook not to come after us."

As Alex drove back to the inn, he marveled at the different hues of Shook posters around town.

No matter what color the poster was, there was no doubt in his mind; Tracy was the only Shook he'd be voting for come Election Day.

10

Alex found Lenora MacLeod waiting for him in the lobby when he got back to Hatteras West. She had her sketch pad tucked under one arm and an expectant expression on her face.

Up until that moment, he'd forgotten completely about their earlier discussion. "Hi, Lenora. Is there something I can help you with?"

"Alex, I hope your answer is yes. I would love for you to pose for me. It shan't take long, I promise."

Alex said, "I'm kind of busy right now. Why don't you get Corki and Jan to pose for you? I bet they'd love to do it."

Lenora said, "It's you I'm interested in, Alex."

"Sorry, I didn't mean to interrupt," Elise said as she came up behind him.

"You're not interrupting anything," Alex said hastily. "If you'll excuse me," he added to Lenora as he followed Elise to the laundry area.

She said, "Alex, you don't have to curtail your conversations around here on my account."

Alex said with a smile, "She just wants me for my body."

Elise shook her head. "That's not funny."

"Hey, I was just teasing." Elise had already run one batch of sheets through the wash and had popped them in the dryer earlier. It was a constant job, washing and folding sheets and towels for their guests. As they worked, he added, "Aren't you going to ask about Emma?"

"I already heard all about it. The mayor was out here again while you were gone. He said he was in town talking to Sandra about raising more money for the covered bridge when you called her."

"What was he doing out here anyway, looking for more donations?"

Elise said, "Ever since he's announced his retirement, Grady's been hovering everywhere. Irma Bean told me he's been hanging out at the restaurant just about every night. Do you want to know the truth? I think the poor man's just lonely."

Alex said, "Don't worry about him. He'll be fine." As Alex took a sheet from the dryer, he said, "Last I heard, Grady's going to do his retirement up in style. He's selling his house and buying a motor home, if you can imagine that. That life might be perfect for him, but I've got to have my roots."

"Sometimes I think about traveling," Elise admitted.

"So where would you go if money were no object?" Alex asked. "France? Ireland? Australia?"

Elise said, "No, there's too much in America I haven't seen. Do you know what I'd really love to do? There are so many wonderful lighthouses in our country; I'd give anything to see them all."

Alex laughed. "You're worse than I am. Do you know where I went on my last vacation?"

"I didn't think you took vacations," Elise said.

"It's tough with the inn and all, but three years ago I shut down for a week and drove to the Outer Banks. I spent all my time haunting the lighthouses out there. I even made a new friend on the coast with his own lighthouse inn."

"I think that's a perfectly sensible vacation."

Alex said, "Tell you what, next time you can go with me."

"Perhaps," Elise said.

"Hey, that wasn't a proposition. I was just making conversation."

Elise bit her lower lip, then said, "Can you finish up here? I just remembered something I need to take care of immediately."

"Absolutely."

After she was gone, Alex wondered what he'd said to set her off. There was no doubt about it. Since their disastrous date, things had taken a decidedly awkward turn between them, and no matter how hard he tried to break the ice dam, he couldn't manage more than chipping a few small chunks away at a time.

Elise came back just as he finished folding the last sheet.

"Your timing is perfect," Alex said. "I just finished."

From the expression on her face, Elise was in no mood for joking. "Alex, something's happened. Somebody just tried to break into Mrs. Nesbitt's room."

Alex said, "In broad daylight?" As he hurriedly left the laundry room, he asked, "What happened?"

"She's in the lobby. You need to talk to her yourself."

As Alex and Elise rushed out into the lobby of the Main Keeper's Quarters, they found Mrs. Nesbitt sipping a cup of hot tea in one of the rockers near the windows in front.

Alex said, "Are you all right?"

She nodded. "Honestly, I hate to be causing such a fuss. It was probably nothing."

Alex took the rocker beside her. "Tell me what happened."

"I was going to go out for a walk, I even got on the path to Bear Rocks, when I suddenly changed my mind and decided a nap would be more in order." She looked apologetic as she added, "I can still do nearly anything I set my mind to, but sometimes I need a little more rest than I used to."

Alex smiled. "I've seen you on your walks. I couldn't keep up with you."

She answered his smile with one of her own. "I know better than that; running an inn is hard work. My sister worked an entire summer at an inn in Nantucket in the fifties."

Elise prompted her. "Tell him what happened."

Mrs. Nesbitt said, "As I said, I decided to rest, so I went back up to my room and stretched out on my bed for a quick nap. I had just fallen asleep when I heard someone trying my doorknob. At first I assumed it was either you or Elise, but you both knock before you try your key. When the door started to open, I'm afraid I screamed."

Alex suddenly went cold. "Are you certain your door was locked when you laid down?"

Mrs. Nesbitt said, "I'm positive. Alex, I'm not about to take a nap with an unlocked door anywhere but in my home."

He patted her hand. "Would you be more comfortable switching rooms? I might be able to talk the newlyweds into swapping with you, if you'd feel more comfortable somewhere else. They mentioned an interest in this building."

She laughed gently. "It will take more than that to drive me out of my favorite room. I'm sure I'll be fine." She sat there a moment, then added, "You know, now that I think about it, perhaps I did forget to latch my door. Yes, I suppose it could have happened that way."

Alex said, "Just in case, I'll take a look at the door and make sure there's nothing wrong with the lock."

She patted his hand. "You're a good man, Alex. Thank you for catering to an old woman's frailty."

Alex looked around the room. "Old woman? Where?"

She laughed again. "Oh, you two are good for me. Now if you'll excuse me, I never did get that nap."

After she was gone, Elise said, "Alex, I've got something to confess."

"You were the one trying to break into her room," he said lightly.

Elise looked grim. "No, but I left my key on the cart, and when I checked on it, it was gone. I swear I wasn't away from it for more than ten seconds."

This was serious business. "Elise, you know you've got to keep that master key with you all the time."

"You don't have to tell me. I made a mistake, Alex." She looked as if she was ready to cry.

"Don't worry, I'm sure it will turn up," he said, trying to reassure her. It would be an expensive process to have Mor or a locksmith retool all the locks at the inn, but if the master key was floating around somewhere, he didn't have any choice.

He added, "Before we do anything rash, let's go see if we can find it."

"Don't you think I looked?" Elise asked. "I was still hunting for it when Mrs. Nesbitt screamed."

"You didn't see anyone nearby, did you?"

"No, but I heard a door slam in the hallway just before I got there," Elise admitted. "I must have just missed whoever it was."

"Who is close by?" Alex asked.

Elise ticked the guests off on her fingers. "Corki and Jan are up in that part of the inn, the newlyweds are there, I just moved them this morning as soon as a room opened up, and Greg and Denise are there, too. I can't imagine any of them trying to break into Mrs. Nesbitt's room. What in the world could anyone want with that sweet old woman?"

"I don't have a clue," Alex admitted.

They walked back to Elise's cart, and Alex glanced down at a load of towels. He reached under one edge and plucked out a tarnished old key on a wrist bungee.

"Is this it?" he asked as he held it up to her.

"You know it is," she said, grabbing the key from him. "Alex, it wasn't here before. I swear it."

Alex said, "There's no chance it could have fallen into the towels when you moved your cart?"

Elise frowned. "I don't think so, but even if it did, how do you explain someone trying to break into Mrs. Nesbitt's room? I don't believe in coincidences, and I know you don't, either."

Alex said, "Well, she said she was trying to take a nap. Is there any chance she dreamed it? I've had some pretty realistic dreams in the past myself."

"I heard the door slam myself, Alex. She didn't dream that. Someone was trying to get into her room."

Alex said, "Tell you what, why don't we keep an eye on her in the meantime. Elise, have you seen anything suspicious about the other folks staying with us?"

"Odd, yes, but suspicious? No, nothing I can put my finger on."

Alex tried to break the tension as he said, "If folks were arrested for being odd, we wouldn't have any guests left at Hatteras West."

Elise wasn't buying it, though. "I still don't like this," she said.

"There's nothing we can do now but keep our eyes open," Alex said.

Alex had been right about the slow grindings of the law. Emma had to spend one night in jail while Sandra worked at securing her release.

At Sandra's urging, he called Mor Pendleton the next day. "Mor, Emma's going to be out this morning. Why don't you go pick her up?"

There was silence on the other end of the line, then Mor said, "I can't make it. Alex, I'm buried with work right now with Les out of town."

Alex said, "You can put that stuff off, Mor, and you know it. Emma needs you."

Mor exploded. "She thinks I killed him, Alex. Can you imagine how that feels?"

Alex said, "Mor, I know you have every right to be upset, but she did it for you."

"That's just it. She was so sure I killed that snake that she confessed to killing him herself."

Alex said, "She knows she made a mistake. There's no doubt in my mind that she'll apologize if you just give her the chance."

There was more silence, then Mor said heavily, "It's too late for that, Alex."

Elise had been standing near the telephone listening to Alex's side of the conversation. As he hung up, she said, "I don't even have to ask how that went. He's pretty upset, isn't he?"

"That's putting it mildly. A friendly face should be there to pick Emma up, don't you think?"

Elise said, "Why don't you go down to the station and take her home? I can handle things here."

"Would you like to go yourself? She might need a shoulder to cry on, and you're better at that than I am. I don't mind doubling up out here."

Elise asked, "Are you sure?"

"Absolutely. Emma needs you right now more than Hatteras West does."

She kissed him on the cheek and said, "Thanks, Alex. I'll try not to be gone too long."

Alex smiled softly to himself after she left. Elise was starting to try to make things right between them again. At least that was something. Blast it all, he still knew in his heart that they belonged together.

So how could he convince her of that?

He'd have plenty of time to think about it during his updated cleaning schedule. There was enough work to keep him busy till twilight.

Greg and Denise, the rockhound couple, checked out of the inn a few minutes before Alex's noon cutoff time. He had to hustle to get their room ready for his next guests, Harry and Barb Rush. The Rushes hadn't said anything about their seven-year-old triplets when they'd made their reservations, or their need for three of the inn's cots.

"Just sign here, Mr. Rush," Alex said as the rambunctious boys carried on a game of "cowboy" in the lobby, each taking turns dying dramatically on the chairs and the floor.

"Boys," Mrs. Rush snapped at them, with absolutely no discernable effect.

Harry Rush said, "They're a little keyed up right now, but don't worry, they're as quiet as cobwebs at night."

Alex knew better, but he kept his comments in check. At least the Rushes were going to be there for just one night.

After he showed them to their room, Alex beat a hasty retreat to the laundry room. It was past two and there was still no sign of Elise. A lunch break had been completely out of the question, and Alex felt his stomach grumbling as he did the laundry. Once everything was going, he stole away to his room just long enough to make a sandwich. When he got back, Alex found that his own master key was suddenly missing.

Alex raced upstairs and found the key in Mrs. Nesbitt's lock, her door standing ajar.

Pushing the door open, Alex felt his pulse pound in his throat. If something had happened to that sweet old lady with his stolen key, Alex would never forgive himself.

The room was blessedly empty; no sign that anything untoward had happened there.

Alex was just leaving the suite when he heard a man's scream of outrage come from the newlyweds' room.

Alex knocked on their door. "What's wrong? It's Alex Winston. Open up."

Paul Jones came to the door, his camera in one hand and a dangling roll of film trailing from the back of his camera.

"What happened?" Alex asked.

"Some juvenile delinquents broke in here while I was in

the bathroom and ruined my film," he said as he held the camera and dangling film aloft.

Mr. Rush opened the door on Alex's first knock. "Sir, I'm afraid one of your boys may have wandered into another guest's room."

His face was ashen at the news. "Oh, no. I'm so sorry. What happened?"

Paul held his camera up. "They trashed my film."

Mr. Rush said, "I'm truly sorry. May I replace it for you?"

"You can't replace the pictures I took," the newlywed said angrily.

Mr. Rush replied, "I don't know what else I can do."

Alex said, "I hate to do this, but—"

Mr. Rush cut him off. "Please don't throw us out. We haven't had a vacation in three years. I'll keep a better eye on them. I promise."

The desperation in the man's voice was overwhelming.

Alex said, "Okay, but I've got to warn you, one more incident and I'm going to have to—"

Rush cut him off again. "I understand. Thanks." He turned to Jones and said, "I really am very sorry."

Alex turned to the newlywed and said, "I'd be happy to buy you another roll of film myself."

The man just grunted as he stomped back into his room, slamming the door in Alex's face.

Alex took his master key and went back to the laundry room, relieved that nothing worse had happened.

11

Mrs. Nesbitt came back from her walk and found Alex in the laundry room.

"You wanted to see me?" she asked as she held aloft the note he'd left her.

"Yes, Ma'am. I don't know how to tell you this, but somebody took my key and used it to get into your room while you were out."

She went white. "Why is this happening, Alex?"

He said, "I wish I knew. Let's go upstairs and see if anything's been disturbed."

After a quick inspection, Mrs. Nesbitt said, "Nothing's out of place. I can't imagine what I could have that anyone else would be interested in."

Alex said, "I don't know what to say. I was careless with my key. Tell you what. I'll be glad to find you other accommodations in Hickory and refund your bill if you'd like."

Mrs. Nesbitt said, "Don't be so melodramatic, Alex, no harm was done here. I'm perfectly content to stay in this room. It has a warm presence that I find somehow comforting."

Alex neglected to mention the fact that a woman had started her descent into suicide in that room, and that another previous tenant had been killed at the top of the lighthouse. If she found comfort there, more power to her. It was one of Alex's favorite rooms as well, despite its troubled history.

Mrs. Nesbitt said, "Don't give it another thought, Alex. I'm sure I'll be quite safe now."

"If you need me any time, call me," Alex said, feeling more concerned about the incident than he cared to admit.

"Posh and tish, I'll be fine."

Regardless of what she said, Alex promised himself to make every effort to ensure the woman's safety while she was staying with him at Hatteras West.

Elise came back to the inn an hour later. From the expression on her face, things had not gone well with Emma.

Alex asked, "Was it as bad as all that?"

Elise said, "Believe me, you don't want to know. I've always thought of Emma as a rock, but this thing has really gotten to her. And Mor still won't talk to her."

"I figured as much. He can be as stubborn as an old goat when he puts his mind to it."

Elise said, "Alex, you've got to talk to him. Emma's tearing herself up with remorse for what she did."

"I tried, remember? He wasn't interested in anything I had to say. The only thing that's going to help Mor is time. He just needs to get over the fact that Emma thought he was capable of murder."

Elise said, "That's not it at all. She was just trying to protect him."

"I know that and you know that, but to Mor, it looks like a real slap in the face. If Emma still needs you, I can manage around here."

Elise shook her head. "After she got all those tears out of her system, she was exhausted. I put her to bed, and I'll be surprised if she doesn't sleep through the night. How are things?"

Alex said, "We've got triplet boys upstairs in Number 5, and they've already managed to destroy the film out of the newlyweds' camera. What in the world made them think it was okay to go into another guest's room?" Alex paused, then added, "That's not all." He hated to confess the new break-in to her. "Somebody was snooping around in Mrs. Nesbitt's room again. They took my key to do it." Before she could say anything, he added, "Don't worry, I found it still in her door. She was out on her walk, but I told her what happened the second she got back. Believe it or not, she wants to stay in that room, after all that's happened."

"What's going on, Alex?"

"I wish I knew," he said.

"It sounds like we're going to have to keep watch on everyone," Elise said.

"We can just add that to the joys of innkeeping," he replied.

Much to Alex's relief, the night passed without further incident. Bright and early the next morning, after tearing through the breakfast line like a herd of wild dogs, the Rushes checked out and were on their way to their next stop. It took Alex and Elise both to clean the room after they were gone. It never ceased to amaze him just how much of a mess some folks could make in one night. Some of his fellow innkeepers had long ago instituted a "no children" rule, but Alex couldn't bring himself to do it. There were too many well-behaved kids out there who loved lighthouses as much as he always had. If it meant suffering through a few stays like the one they'd had the night before, it was worth it.

At least that's what he kept telling himself as he scraped modeling clay off the honey-toned hardwood floor.

Things were quiet around the inn over the next few days. Alex and Elise managed to slip back into some of their old routines, but there was no doubt something subtle had changed between them. Where there'd been light banter between them before, there was now a forced formality that Alex had tried in vain to ease. He seriously considered turning the lighthouse beacon on again, just to see one of Elise's smiles.

The phone rang while Alex was dusting the front desk, and he answered before it had a chance to finish its first ring.

"The Hatteras West Inn," he answered automatically.

"Alex, this is Doc Drake. Has the sheriff called you yet?"

Alex prepared himself for the worse. "No, what's happened now?"

"Relax, this is about the Sturbridge case. The medical examiner in Raleigh finally figured out what happened to Emma's ex-husband, but it took him some time. You'll never guess what killed Sturbridge."

Alex said, "I don't have a clue."

"A blow to the chest, plain and simple. Evidently Sturbridge was a ticking time bomb waiting to go off. The medical examiner said it was amazing the man lived as long as he did, given the weakened condition of his heart. One shove put him over the edge."

Alex asked, "Would it have had to be hard enough to leave a bruise?"

Drake sighed. "Not necessarily, but in this case it left a small one. I missed it, Alex. Sturbridge had a tattoo of a mermaid on his chest, and the tail obscured the bruise. I've never seen anything like it."

"So what happened?"

"The way it plays out, Sturbridge must have received a blow to the chest, hard enough to stop his heart in its weakened condition, and that was that. It's a pretty clear case of heart failure."

"It almost sounds like he died of natural causes," Alex said.

"Don't kid yourself. I'm not saying it was intentional, but whoever killed him might as well have put a gun to the man's head. It's still murder, no matter how you look at it. Alex, do me a favor, would you?"

"Anything," Alex said.

"Have the decency to act surprised when Armstrong tells you all this later."

Alex quickly agreed. "I promise. And Doc? Thanks for calling me."

"I thought you'd like to know."

After Alex hung up, he couldn't keep his mind off the way Toby Sturbridge had died. When he'd assumed it had been some exotic poison or even just natural causes, Alex had been certain Mor had nothing to do with it.

But a blow to the chest was something else entirely.

He hated the idea, but Alex could easily see Mor giving Sturbridge a punch to the chest to make his point. As Drake had said, it wouldn't even have had to be that hard, given the man's condition.

But it was still murder.

And it was looking more and more possible that his best friend in the world might have done it after all.

The next day Alex got an early morning telephone call as he was putting out the breakfast bar.

As soon as he heard Sally Anne's voice, Alex asked her to hold on and said, "Elise, can you spare me for a minute?"

"I can handle this, Alex," she said.

Once he was away from Elise and their guests, he asked Sally Anne, "So what's up? I figured you'd be jammed with your breakfast crowd." He could hear the noises of the full diner in the background.

"I just had to call and give you an update," she said. "Conner Shook just left. He's got some kind of bomb he's dropping on Tracy tonight at the debate. I don't know what it is, but he was pretty smug about it when he was talking to Dad."

"Did you call Tracy and tell her? I don't know if she's

still home, but if she's not there, you could try her at Shantara's."

"Both lines were busy," Sally Anne said.

"They're probably talking to each other. Why don't you try them and I'll see if I can get through later myself. Anything else?" Alex asked.

"Let's see, I heard that Luanne Trist is pregnant, Don Rainer made a big donation to your Bridge Committee, oh, and Emma and Mor are on the skids, but you probably already knew that. The biggest thing is that Oxford Hitchcock had a fight with his lady friend in Lenoir right before he died. The sheriff's going over there this afternoon to talk to her."

For a small town, a lot seemed to be happening around Elkton Falls. "Thanks for keeping me up to speed, Sally Anne."

She paused, then said, "There's something I'm forgetting. Oh yeah, Irma Bean's all up in arms about a new restaurant coming to town. She was trying to get Dad upset, but he's not all that worried. He says they won't be competition for us, but Irma's frantic." In the background, Alex heard Buck yell, "Sally Anne."

"I've got to go. I'll call later, Alex," she said as she hung up.

Alex thought about what Sally Anne had said as he helped Elise clean up after their guests were through with their meals.

"No bad news, I hope," Elise said.

Alex emptied the trash. "I'm not sure what to make of it. It turns out Oxford had a fight with his female companion not long before he was murdered. The sheriff's going to talk with her this afternoon."

"And you'd love to go with him, wouldn't you? It's okay with me if you can talk him into it."

Alex said, "I appreciate the offer, but I know Armstrong. He's not going to want me horning in on any of his investigations any more than I already am. No, I'll stay here and clean the inn with you."

They split up, as was becoming their custom, and tackled most of the rooms before lunch. Alex was speaking with a travel agent from England about a tour stopping at the inn when Jan and Corki approached the desk, their bags in their hands. The phone call quickly wrapped up, and Alex said, "I forgot you ladies were leaving us today."

Corki said, "We're off to another inn."

Jan added with a twinkle in her eye, "And another souvenir. I'm not entirely certain the Grove Park really qualifies as an inn, despite its name. What am I saying? Who cares? I'm getting a massage tonight."

Alex knew the Grove Park Inn in Asheville was a truly elegant place, and he shuddered when he thought about the comparisons the ladies would be making that night. "I'm sure you'll have a wonderful time."

"Your lighthouse will be tough to beat," Corki said. "It was especially nice of you to turn the light on just for us."

Alex grinned. "I just wish I could do it every night. I'm glad you enjoyed it."

After the ladies were on their way, Alex figured it would be the perfect time to clean their room, even though there were no new guests scheduled until the next day. He found Elise finishing up Mrs. Nesbitt's room.

"Why don't we knock this one out together," he said as he opened the door to Jan and Corki's room. Elise nodded and started on the bathroom while Alex dust-mopped the honeyed hardwood floor under the bed.

There was something under his mop; he could hear it skitter across the floor as he drew it to him.

There, along with a wrapper for a candy bar and a torn postcard of the inn, Alex found one of the *A*'s from his Scrabble game. Either the ladies had lost one of their own tiles there, or Hatteras West had been victimized by another letter thief. If it was from his game, at least there would be one *A* left for those daring enough to play with a modified pool of letters. He trotted downstairs, and sure enough, the rest of the *A*'s were gone.

When he got back to the room, Elise said, "Where did you run off to?"

"I found a tile from our Scrabble game under the bed. Our game now has just one *A*."

Elise said, "I guess you'll have to get Mor to make you more. Jan and Corki probably think it's hilarious after the story about the original letter theft. I found this while you were gone." Inside an envelope with his name on it, Alex read the note from Corki explaining the theft, along with a ten-dollar bill to replace the game.

Alex said, "It's amazing what some people will take from the inn as a souvenir. You never can tell, can you?" Alex added, "I probably should give Mor a call to see how he's doing. He's got to get over this and speak to Emma again. I know it's tearing them both apart."

He looked at Elise and could see that she wanted to say something, but she was holding back. Alex said, "Listen, I know it's probably not any of my business, but they're my friends and I hate to see this all fall apart."

"Alex, I love that you're trying, but you can't fix everything."

"I've got to at least try."

Elise said, "You're a true romantic, aren't you?"

He gestured out to the lighthouse, built by his forefather as a tribute to love, and said, "What can I say? It runs in the family. The only thing I feel bad about is leaving you here alone so much."

"I'm getting used to it," she said, adding a grin to ease the jab in her words. "Honestly, I can handle it, we've already finished the lion's share of the work. Now shoo."

Alex left the last bits of cleaning to her and promised to be back in time to help with the daily laundry.

While it was true he wanted a chance to talk to his best friend, there was more motive behind his actions than his role as Cupid.

Alex had to know if it was possible Mor had killed Sturbridge, whether it had been the intended result or not.

12

With Lester Williamson out of town, Alex knew he was taking a long shot going by Mor or Les's, but the handyman had to go back for tools and parts sooner or later, and Alex hoped to catch him at the shop, where they could talk uninterrupted.

Mor was behind the counter, nibbling on a sandwich as he browsed through one of Les's many magazines.

"Funny, you don't strike me as the type to read *Architectural Digest*," Alex said.

"It's better than *Modern Bride*. I can't imagine what Les was thinking when he ordered that one."

Alex said, "He's got an addiction, there's no doubt about it. You know how the schoolkids flock to him when they're selling magazine subscriptions, and he doesn't have the heart to say no. Speaking of modern brides, have you talked to Emma lately?"

Mor pushed his sandwich way. "Alex, I know you mean well, but don't."

"Don't what?" Alex tried to ask as innocently as he could manage.

"Don't butt in," Mor said. The two of them had been

friends for so long that bluntness had long been one of the
cornerstones of their relationship.

Alex said, "Okay, I won't say what a pigheaded mon-
key you're being about all this, and how you should be
honored somebody would be willing to go to jail for you.
I won't even say how I doubt there's another soul in the
world willing to do that, and that includes me."

Mor said, "For somebody who's not going to say anything, you're doing an awful lot of talking."

Alex said, "What can I say, I'm a master noncommuni-
cator."

"Since you're so all fired up to discuss my love life,
let's talk about yours. You never did tell me what happened
between you and Elise on your big date."

"There's nothing to tell," Alex admitted, uneasy with
the spotlight turned back on him.

"Come on, Buddy, I know better than that. What happened?"

Alex said, "You want to know the truth? It was a disaster, from start to finish. I'm surprised she's even still talking to me."

"You didn't do anything stupid, did you?" Mor asked.

"No, not what you're thinking, but I surely made plenty
of mistakes."

Mor finished his sandwich with one bite, took a swig of
chocolate milk, then said, "Did anything happen that can't
be fixed?"

"That's kind of what I wanted to know about you and
Emma," Alex said, holding his ground.

Mor seemed to think about it, then shrugged. "I'll get
over it. I've gotta tell you, it stings to have her think I
could do something like that."

Alex knew he had to tread lightly now. He said, "It's
hard to believe he died waiting for you in your truck. Listen, I understand if you didn't want to tell Armstrong, but
are you sure you didn't speak to him before you found
him?"

Mor stood, and Alex realized yet again just how physi-
cally powerful his friend was. Intimidation alone would

stop most men from pushing, but the two of them had been friends too long for Alex to let that happen.

Mor said, "I told him the truth, Alex. I didn't say 'Boo' to the man, and I surely didn't lay a hand on Toby Sturbridge, not that I wouldn't have been tempted if I'd known he was here."

Alex nodded. "That's good enough for me."

"I'm so glad you believe me," Mor said sarcastically as he wadded up the wrapper from his sandwich and shot it at the trash can. It ricocheted off an old-fashioned jukebox waiting for parts and trickled lamely into the can.

"Bank shot," Mor called out after the fact.

Looking for some way to end their conversation on a better note, Alex asked, "Hey, are you going to the debate tonight?"

Mor said, "Are you kidding? It's going to be better than anything on television, that's for sure. I'm getting there early so I can get a good seat."

"I'll see you there, then. Save me a spot. And Mor, think about what I didn't say."

Mor nodded. "I'll try my best not to."

As Alex left, he realized he'd done all he could. Now it was up to Mor to swallow the remnants of his hurt pride and move on with his life.

That was one thing Alex couldn't do for him.

While he was in town, Alex decided he might as well go by Armstrong's office and see if he'd gotten back from his interview with Oxford's lady friend. Maybe he'd found something to divert his suspicion away from Tracy. With the election just around the corner, any kind of cloud over her candidacy could spell disaster for her and put Conner Shook in the mayor's office.

The sheriff was at his desk, frowning at a stack of papers in front of him. Alex could sympathize. As an innkeeper, sometimes he felt he was drowning in paperwork, and he didn't have to deal with nearly as much bureaucracy as the sheriff must have faced every day.

"Sometimes it's tough remembering the color of your desktop, isn't it," Alex asked.

The sheriff nodded. "It's been so long since I've seen it, I don't even think I'd recognize it if it reared up and bit me on the tail."

Alex sat in the chair across from the sheriff and said, "Have you got a second? I'd like to talk to you."

Armstrong leaned back in his chair and said, "Yeah, I've been meaning to come back out to the inn, but things have been a little crazy around here lately."

"What's on your mind?" Alex asked.

The sheriff riffled through the papers, then pulled out an official-looking document with the North Carolina state seal on it. He tossed it at Alex, then said, "It's the report from the medical examiner in Raleigh. Sturbridge died from a blow to the chest."

Alex caught himself before he admitted he already had that particular bit of information. He studied the report, then said, "It looks like it didn't take much, did it?"

Armstrong said, "No, but any way you cut it, it's still murder."

"So what are you going to do now?"

The sheriff said, "I'm not going to bother sitting down with Emma Sturbridge and Mor Pendleton and talking. Sandra won't let them say a word. I've got to dig into it a little deeper before I approach anybody else."

Alex said lightly, "I heard a rumor that you were going to talk with Oxford Hitchcock's girlfriend today. Any luck with her?"

Armstrong snapped, "I swear this town needs something to do besides keeping tabs on me. Yeah, I talked to her, but she's in the clear."

Alex said, "That must have been some alibi."

The sheriff nodded. "She was in Hickory getting an emergency appendectomy the night Oxford was murdered. That's as good as it gets in my book."

"So you're back to square one on that case," Alex asked.

"Alex Winston, are you telling me you're butting your nose into two of my investigations?"

Alex admitted, "Tracy asked me to keep my eyes open, and that's what I'm doing. I'm not trying to interfere at all, Sheriff. Trust me. I've got enough on my plate as it is."

That seemed to mollify the sheriff somewhat. "Tracy Shook frets too much, she always has. You'd think she'd be occupied with this big debate tonight instead of worrying about what I'm up to."

"To be honest with you, she's probably worried about both."

The sheriff said, "She'd better focus on Conner, at least for tonight. I was at the barbershop this morning and he was getting a trim. Man, that guy holds a grudge. He's been telling everyone in sight that he's coming after his ex-wife with both guns blazing."

Alex suddenly had a thought. "Have you considered the possibility that Conner might have had something to do with Oxford's murder?"

Armstrong looked surprised by the prospect. "You think he might have killed his own candidate? Why would he do that, Alex, when everybody knew Oxford was in the lead in the race? He was looking like a shoo-in."

Alex said, "Maybe he wanted to beat Tracy himself. Or maybe there was more going on there than anybody knows about. He could have his own reasons."

"I've talked to him a little about the case, and he didn't strike me as that likely a suspect," the sheriff admitted.

"I wouldn't write him off just yet," Alex said. "There could be more there than meets the eye."

Armstrong just shrugged as his telephone rang. "Excuse me, Alex, I've got to take this. I've been waiting for a call from Raleigh all afternoon."

After that, there was nothing else he could think to do. Alex left the station and headed back to the inn. It was time to work at his real job and leave the detecting to the professionals.

Later that night, Alex heard a voice beckon him near the front of the auditorium as he walked into the cavernous place. "Hey, I thought you'd be here with Elise," Mor said as he made room for Alex. "I saved two seats for you guys."

"She didn't feel right leaving our guests alone," Alex admitted. "I know you still haven't called Emma, or she wouldn't be out at Hatteras West keeping Elise company. They're listening to it on the radio together."

Mor shook his head. "That's not going to be nearly as good. Radio's no good for this. You can't see the flinches, the flushed faces, or smell the fear in the air.".

Alex asked, "So who are you supporting anyway?"

Mor smiled. "I was thinking about writing your name in on my ballot."

Alex said, "Tell you what, I'll make you a deal. I won't vote for you if you don't vote for me."

Irma Bean brushed past them as Alex called out to her. He said, "I can't believe it. Irma Bean isn't at her restaurant at night?"

Irma said, "Who let you two boys out on your own? I'm looking for Mrs. Hurley. We were supposed to meet here ten minutes ago." Mrs. Hurley was a retired schoolteacher who taught several night classes at the community college. Mor and Alex had both taken classes from her, though Mor had had more free time in his evenings until Emma Sturbridge had come along.

"I haven't seen her in donkey years," Mor said. "But you're always welcome to sit with us."

Irma smiled. "I don't know if my reputation could stand the strain."

Alex said, "Seriously, is this debate important enough to get you to shut down for the night?"

"My staff's working, so we're open as usual, but they'll have to do without me tonight. This election is more important than feeding people," she said in a lowered voice. "We've got to get that girl elected."

Mor said, "Irma, I never thought of you as all that political."

"Mor Pendleton, there's a lot you don't know about me."

"No doubt about that," he said. They spotted Mrs. Hurley come in through the back, and Irma said, "Excuse me, gentlemen, there she is."

The high school auditorium filled up quickly, and soon it was time for the debate to begin. Grady Hatch took the stage first, raised his hands for silence, then began.

"Folks, I want to thank you for coming out tonight. Give yourselves a big hand."

Most folks were happy for an excuse to do something, even if it was nothing more than clapping for themselves.

After the applause died down, Grady said, "I don't have to introduce tonight's combatants, I mean candidates." There was a snicker from the crowd at his slip of the tongue.

"Most likely there's no need to go into long, fancy bios of the Shooks, you've known them both all their lives. Conner, Tracy, let's get this rascal started."

Conner and Tracy Shook entered the stage from different sides, barely making eye contact as they walked to the identical podiums separated by the moderator's table. Conner wore a suit that must have cost him a fortune, while Tracy chose a pants suit like the ones women politicos in Washington seemed to favor Alex thought it was funny that Conner was standing behind a podium draped with Tracy's colors, while she was behind his. It took them both a full second to realize their mistake, then they awkwardly changed sides like tennis players crossing the net.

Alex was afraid the mayor was going to botch the moderator's job, and he was relieved when Ernest Faith, a newsman from one of the Charlotte television stations, took a seat behind the desk. Grady slipped off into the wings, no doubt to get away from the heat of the battle, then walked down one side of the aisle to the back of the auditorium, where it was standing room only. It was quite a turnout for Elkton Falls.

Ernest gave the audience his well-practiced smile and said, "Welcome. I'd like to start tonight's debate by giving each candidate the opportunity to tell the audience why they should be Mayor of Elkton Falls. Both candidates have decided that in order to avoid confusion, we will be using first names only during this debate." That got a snicker out of the audience. When it died, the newsman continued, "We flipped a coin backstage, and Tracy won. Tracy?"

She looked nervous, staring down at her notes before she made eye contact with the audience. The silence grew on without a word from the candidate, and the crowd started getting restless.

Ernest said again, "Tracy?"

She took a deep gulp of air, then said, "Thank you. I'm running for mayor because I want to make a difference. Mayor Hatch has been doing a decent job, but I feel we need a new, strong leadership to keep the developers in check, to assure the high standards we are used to having here, and to lead our town into growth slowly and with careful consideration. I want to keep Elkton Falls the way it should be: filled with heart, with friendship, and with good neighbors."

She looked relieved to be finished, and the crowd dutifully applauded.

Ernest waited a moment, then said, "Now Conner."

Conner shot a look at Tracy, then turned his brightest smile onto the audience. "Folks, my ex-wife has offered you a Mayberry ideal. Well, Mayberry was on TV. This is real life. Elkton Falls needs growth to sustain itself. New jobs, new people moving in, this all represents more for all of us as we expand our tax base. We shouldn't be discouraging expansion, we should be encouraging it. Tracy, the fifties have been over a long time. We need someone who's looking toward tomorrow, not living in yesterday."

There was a louder round of applause than Alex had hoped for. Conner had taken Tracy's words and wrapped them around her throat. He was much smoother, more polished than Tracy, with his ready smile and sharp delivery.

And it looked to Alex as if the residents of Elkton Falls were eating it up.

At one point, Tracy looked as if she was going to take off after Conner right there on stage, his remarks were so inflammatory, but she kept her temper and instead jabbed back at him with a few shots of her own.

After the summations at the very end of the debate, both candidates looked as if they'd gone through a battle.

And for the life of him, Alex couldn't figure out who had won.

Mor stood as the candidates made their way out the back of the auditorium to swing around and greet folks as they left. "Well, that was something."

"Did any of it change your mind at all?" Alex asked.

"No, but I doubt anything will. These two were preaching to their own choirs all night long. Conner's pushing for expansion, and Tracy wants things to stay the way they are. It should make for an interesting election on Tuesday."

"It should," Alex agreed.

He and Mor were still standing there chatting when they both heard the scream behind them.

Someone at the back of the auditorium was in trouble.

13

Mor and Alex rushed backstage just in time to see Tracy faint. Conner, obviously uncomfortable with his ex-wife in his arms, said, "Somebody get a doctor."

"What happened?" Alex asked as Mor left to find Doc Drake.

"That did," Conner said, gesturing with his head toward the back door.

There, hanging from the rafters, was a female mannequin dressed in something just like Tracy would wear, with a sign around its neck.

DROP OUT OR DIE.

At that moment, a flash went off behind Alex, then another.

He looked toward the light and saw Max Logan from the *Elkton Falls Journal* running back up the aisle, his camera in his hand.

"Great," Conner said. "It's not exactly how I wanted to get in the papers."

Tracy started to come around. Her eyelids fluttered, then she looked startled to find herself in Conner's arms.

"Let go of me," she said angrily.

Conner released her and said, "If you want to break your tailbone, that's fine with me."

Alex reached out and gave Tracy a hand, and she wobbled slightly as she stood, leaning into Alex so she wouldn't fall.

Evidently when the photographer saw that no one was chasing him, he decided to come back for more shots.

Alex said, "Come on, Max, it's not fair taking advantage of Tracy like this."

Logan said, "Are you kidding me? This is Page One stuff. I've got a shot of the hanging body and Tracy passed out under it."

"It's a mannequin, somebody's idea of a dirty trick. You've got more class than that," he said.

Max said, "It's not a question of class, this is real news."

Alex turned to Conner. "Aren't you going to try to stop him?"

Conner said halfheartedly, "What can I do about it? Logan's right; we can't keep the newspaper from publishing something just because we don't like the subject matter."

As Max raced out of the auditorium, Tracy snapped, "You think this is something positive? How are your old buddies and new girlfriends going to feel when you're seen holding me on the front page tomorrow?"

Conner smiled. "Go with the flow, Trace. Remember, any press is good press."

Tracy pointed to the dummy. "Is this your idea of a joke, Conner?"

He frowned. "Come on, you know me better than that. I'm going to whip your tail fair and square. You don't actually think I want you to drop out, do you?"

After Conner was gone, Alex asked her, "Do you believe him?"

"I hate to admit it, but this isn't Conner's style. Now if he'd come after me with a knife or tried to run me over with his car, maybe. He doesn't have the aptitude for psychological warfare."

Alex inadvertently brushed against the dummy, and the legs swung eerily back and forth. "I think you'd better take this threat seriously."

"And give Conner the satisfaction of a walkover election? I'd rather die first."

There was no doubt about the sincerity in her voice. Alex was about to say something else when Mor rushed back. "Doc's delivering a baby over in Viewmont. Do you want me to call 911?"

Tracy said, "That's all I need to sink my chances, a ride in the ambulance because the 'poor little woman' couldn't take a prank. I'm fine. Excuse me, guys, but I'd better head over to Shantara's and see what we can do about this mess."

"You aren't even going to call the sheriff?" Alex asked.

"What's he going to do, follow me around between now and the election? I don't need a bodyguard, Alex. I'll be fine."

That left Alex and Mor standing in the wings, studying the dummy.

"Should we at least cut it down?" Mor asked.

"I don't know, maybe we should call the sheriff before we do anything."

From the aisle, they heard a familiar voice say, "No need, I'm already here."

Mor looked strained as the sheriff approached. Armstrong said, "I heard about this outside. What happened?"

"Somebody's idea of a bad joke," Alex said, respecting Tracy's wish not to make a big deal of it.

"I don't think it's all that funny," the sheriff said as he tugged on one leg, which promptly came off in his hand. He stared at a second, then dropped it to the floor. It was obvious Mor was choking back laughter, and Armstrong was too sharp to miss it.

"You think this is funny," he said angrily.

"The dummy or the leg?" Mor asked.

Armstrong said, "If I were you, I wouldn't be joking around about anything. I'm not done with you, Mister."

"You know where I am," Mor said. "See you later, Alex."

As Armstrong watched Mor go, Alex found the rope holding up the dummy tied off to the side. He said, "Sheriff, should I lower it to the floor?"

"Yeah, you'all are probably right; it's got to be some kind of prank. I swear, kids have way too much time on their hands these days."

Alex untied the rope and the dummy eased to the floor. He nudged the hand-printed sign with his toe. Blast it all, he couldn't just let it go. If something happened to Tracy because he hadn't made a fuss about this, Alex would never forgive himself.

He said, "Sheriff, maybe you should have one of your deputies keep an eye on Tracy, at least until Election Day."

Armstrong shook his head. "I wish I could, but I'm not running the Secret Service, Alex. I don't have the manpower or the budget to protect either candidate."

"This could be serious," Alex pressed.

"Tell you what, I'll have some of the boys keep an eye on her house when they're out on patrol. Does that satisfy you?"

"I know it's the best you can do with what you've got," Alex said. "So what do we do about this?"

Armstrong said, "Let the stage manager deal with it. It's most likely his dummy anyway."

Alex retrieved the sign. "Shouldn't we at least have this checked for fingerprints?"

Armstrong said, "What's this 'we' business? There's nothing here to investigate, and you're not a cop, Alex."

The innkeeper tucked the sign under one arm and said, "Then I'm taking it with me, if you don't mind."

"Suit yourself," Armstrong said. "Come on, Alex, I'll walk you out."

Alex followed him out of the auditorium, still wondering about the seriousness of the threat against Tracy. Maybe he could convince her to come out to the inn and stay until after the election. At least there he could keep an eye on her.

It was worth a shot.

Back at the inn, Alex found Elise alone in the lobby of the Main Keeper's Quarters. "Where's Emma?" he asked. "I thought she was listening to the debate with you."

"She just left. She decided she couldn't stand it any-more and went over to Mor's to try to patch things up," Elise admitted.

"Emma needs to give him some space," Alex said. "He's not ready to talk about this yet."

Elise said, "He might not be ready, but Emma's dying inside." She pointed to the sign under his arm. "What's that?"

Alex held it up by its edges for her to read. Elise said, "Where on earth did you find it?"

"It was hanging around a dummy's neck backstage of the auditorium. The mannequin was dressed up to look like Tracy. Conner swears he didn't do it, but I'm not sure I be-lieve him."

Elise sat back on the sofa. "What did Tracy do when she found it?"

"She fainted. Good old Conner was right there to catch her, too."

Elise frowned. "That poor woman."

"You don't know the half of it. Max Logan got a picture of Tracy fainting dead away into Conner's arms with the dummy hanging in the background."

Elise said, "That's terrible, especially after the debate went so well for her."

Alex stoked the fire, then said, "Do you really think she did all that well? I hate to admit it, but I thought Conner did some real damage, and there was her hesitation there at the start. It was kind of rough on her."

Elise said, "What hesitation? We didn't hear anything on the radio. They lost the feed right after Grady intro-duced them, but it came back just as Tracy started her opening remarks. I still think she handled herself ex-tremely well."

So the radio station had lost her hesitation altogether. Alex wondered how the visual of the debate could be so different from the audio alone, then he remembered stories of the Kennedy-Nixon debate on television. His folks had told him that the people who heard it on the radio thought Nixon won, while the television viewers gave the nod to Kennedy. Maybe her stilted beginning hadn't crushed Tracy's candidacy after all.

Then he remembered the photograph, and the mannequin. When word got out what had happened, it would most likely ruin the last of her chances, and Alex didn't relish the idea of Conner Shook being the mayor of Elkton Falls for the next two years.

Alex had just gone to bed when there was a frantic knocking on his door. As an innkeeper, he was used to being awakened at all hours of the night. Pulling on the robe by his bed, he was startled to see Greg and Denise, the two rockhounds who had checked out the day before.

Denise looked frantic, to the point of tears.

Alex asked, "What's wrong?" fearing the worst.

She said, "My ring. It's gone. Did you find it? Is it here?"

Greg added, "It's a three-and-a-half-carat Russian Alexandrite stone set in Mexican gold. It's worth a small fortune."

Denise said, "It's more than that. It's my engagement ring."

Alex said, "I'm sorry, I didn't see it when I was cleaning yesterday. I don't know how to tell you this, but we had some other folks stay in that room last night."

"Oh, no." Denise looked shattered.

Alex said, "Let's go upstairs and check anyway. We might have missed it."

"I can't believe it's gone," Denise said.

Greg tried to comfort his wife. "It's probably still up there, Honey. We'll find it."

Alex had his doubts, but he kept them to himself. He grabbed his master key and they went upstairs. Thirty minutes later they'd torn the room apart, but still no ring.

Alex was about to admit it was a lost cause when he

saw something glittering on an old iron filigree hanging on the wall that served as a curtain stay. He walked over, and to his amazement, it was indeed the missing ring.

Denise hugged him when he presented it to her. "You're a genius. Where was it?"

Alex showed the couple where it had been. Denise said, "I remember now. I took it off to take a bath, then Greg, you called me from the other room. I put it there so I wouldn't forget it, if you can believe that."

Greg smiled. "Sure, blame the husband, take the easy way out."

Alex surveyed the mess they'd created and said, "It's getting too late to drive anywhere and the room's free for the night. Let me get this cleaned up and you're welcome to spend the night here, with my compliments."

Denise said, "We'd love to, but friends are expecting us in Charlotte tonight. We'll stay and help clean up before we go, though."

Alex shook his head. "I can handle this. Why don't you two go ahead? And enjoy the rest of your vacation."

"Oh, we will," Denise said happily. "And we're even going to come back next year."

Greg said, "Thanks, Alex. I can't tell you how much this means to us."

Elise showed up as Greg and Denise were leaving.

"What happened?" she asked.

"Denise lost her engagement ring, but the panic is over. We found it."

She followed Alex back upstairs, and they had the room back in neat order in no time.

Elise said, "There's never a dull moment around here, is there? Good night."

"Good night," Alex answered, though he had hoped their late night proximity would ease some of the discomfort between them.

No such luck.

It appeared that the damage they'd done was irreversible.

14

"Well, the celebrity arrives," Elise said as Alex walked into the lobby the next morning.

"What are you talking about?" Alex asked.

She showed him the newspaper, and he was appalled to see that Logan, that newshound, had used two of the shots he'd taken in the auditorium. Side by side, there were photos of Tracy fainted dead away in Conner's arms, and then one with the hanged dummy leering down at them. Alex was in one corner of the first photo, reaching a hand out to Tracy.

Blast it all! "I can't believe he'd stoop to this kind of journalism," Alex said.

Elise said, "The caption's almost as bad as the photographs are."

Alex looked at the bold headlines and felt his face grow hot.

It said, FAINTING CANDIDATE NEEDS DIFFERENT KIND OF SUPPORT in screaming black letters.

Oh, no. Alex couldn't believe the part the newspaper was playing in destroying the last shred of hope for Tracy's campaign.

"Listen, she was the victim here," Alex said.

"Don't you think I realize that, Alex? Everybody who matters knows that Tracy had every right to be frightened. Still, the picture of her passed out in Conner's arms isn't going to help matters. Elkton Falls is a pretty conservative place."

"What about Conner? It could hurt him too, couldn't it?"

Elise shook her head. "It's pretty obvious the paper's backing him. The story implies that he was just caring for his ex-wife in her time of need. It makes Tracy look like some kind of weakling, though not in words that are that obvious. No, they've done a masterful job on her."

Alex said, "I won't stand for it. There's got to be something I can do."

The phone rang, and Alex grabbed it.

Mor was on the other end. "Hey, Alex. That press coverage was pretty bad, wasn't it?"

"You saw the paper," Alex said.

"Man, everybody in Elkton Falls saw it. I was over at Buck's for breakfast. You wouldn't believe the buzzing. It sounded like somebody let a hive loose in there."

"Are the reactions all bad?" Alex asked, already afraid he knew the answer.

"Not from what I heard. Sounds to me like folks are pretty evenly split. I don't think the newspaper fooled them, or swayed anybody at all. The kudzu vine had already spread the truth about the real story about the mannequin, and folks are pretty riled up about the newspaper painting Tracy so badly. It actually might have helped her, to be honest with you. Nobody likes a bully."

Alex said, "That's the best news I've heard all day. Keep your ears open, would you?"

"I can't help myself," he said before hanging up.

Elise asked, "Who was that?"

"Mor was reporting in from the diner. Seems the smear might have backfired. Tracy's still in the running."

Elise nodded. "I'm glad to hear it. Now I'd better get

started on Dual. And Alex . . ." she added, her voice trailing off.

"Yes?" he asked.

"I know you want to rake the newspaper editors and the photographer who took those pictures over the coals, but don't. We don't need any more bad publicity for the inn, do we?" Her words were softened with a smile.

"I promise, I'll do my best to be good."

"That's the spirit," she said.

Another crisis averted, he thought to himself as he started cleaning up after the breakfast bar.

But Alex knew the day was still young, and there was a lot more time for mischief before the sun set.

Alex was checking over the guest register, wondering how they were going to keep the inn full now that they were back to full capacity. Advertising was a necessary evil, since his word-of-mouth trade wasn't enough to keep them fully booked, but it was a part of the job Alex really didn't care for. It was frustrating knowing that part of his budget for ads was wasted. If he was being honest with himself, what really bothered him was that he couldn't know for sure which ads worked and which didn't, even using the suite number ploy on the return address. Truth be told, most folks forgot to include his carefully disguised tracking information when they made their reservations.

Lenora approached with a sketchbook under one arm and asked, "Why the frown, Alex?"

"Nothing, it's just the innkeeper's scourge; paperwork," he said, trying to ease the tension in his face.

She nodded. "What you need is some fresh air. How about a thirty-minute break so I can make a few quick sketches?"

"You're relentless, you know that, don't you?"

Lenora smiled softly. "When it's important to me, I certainly can be."

Alex shrugged. "Okay, but I can only give you fifteen minutes. I mean it, that's it."

"I'll gladly take whatever I can get," she said.

Alex thought about tracking Elise down to tell her where he would be, but he finally decided he was just too embarrassed to admit that he'd be away from his duties so he could model.

He settled for a sign on the desk that said BACK SOON, and they went outside.

"Where would you like to do this, the top of the lighthouse?" he asked.

"Not today. The light should be perfect at Bear Rocks for our session."

"Suits me," Alex said. Bear Rocks was a part of Winston land, an outcropping of granite worn away by erosion, leaving shoots, slides, and passageways through the rocks. Next to the lighthouse, it was his favorite place on Earth. How lucky he was to have both at his doorstep, even luckier that he owned them. It was time yet again for him to count his blessings. He had his health, his family land, and friends he cared about.

Lenora broke into his thoughts. "You're quiet today. Anything I can help you with? I'm told I'm easy to talk to."

"No, everything's fine," he said as they cut through the path that connected Bear Rocks to the lighthouse and inn area. Alex owed its neatly sculpted condition to an amateur landscaper, a man who had transformed the grounds of Hatteras West into a garden spot, and Alex missed the man's deft touch with a pair of pruning shears. He knew that it wouldn't be long before the wildness of the place began to grow back.

"You and Elise are having your own problems, aren't you?" Lenora asked. Her question was soft, but the inflection showed she cared about his answer.

"I guess we were both expecting too much," he admitted. Usually it was other people who opened up to Alex, but this woman had an empathy in her that startled him. After she had him posed on Mamma Bear, one of his favorite formations that formed a cradle for the warming sun, Alex found himself telling Lenora all about his history with Elise. There was none of that foolishness about keeping deadly still, and Alex found himself forgetting that he was even posing, he was so engrossed in telling her all that had transpired between him and Elise since she'd first come to Hatteras West in the back of Sheriff Armstrong's squad car looking for work as a maid.

Finally, as Lenora put a last stroke onto the paper, she said, "Alex, it's difficult changing a relationship once it's established, but there's one thing you must remember."

"What's that?" he asked.

"It's not impossible. You just have to be patient."

He nodded. "That's what Elise has been telling me, but I'm beginning to have my doubts."

She laughed. "Doubts are for the weak of heart, Alex, and you're certainly not that. Sometimes it's hard for a man of action to simply wait."

Lenora sketched some more, then said, "Your mayor certainly likes to tour Elkton Falls, doesn't he?"

"Yeah, Grady's been everywhere lately. Why, where did you see him?"

"Just yesterday I was out at your pond sketching some waterfowl, and I saw him deep in conversation with another man. I didn't recognize him until I saw today's paper. I believe it was Conner Shook, and from the look of things at the pond, the two of them weren't exactly getting along."

Alex said, "Conner could make a teddy bear mad."

"The mayor was not happy, I can agree with that. He seemed intimidated."

Alex said, "I bet I know why. Grady promised to stay out of the mayoral race, but it sounds as though Conner's putting pressure on him for an endorsement. Tracy told me he probably would once he took over the nomination."

"That's why I stay away from the political world," Lenora said as she pondered adding a line, then put her charcoal down. "It is a field of endeavor founded on confrontation."

Alex glanced at his watch and said, "We've been out

here almost an hour! I can't believe how quickly the time passed."

"So you'll pose for me again before I leave?"

Alex smiled. "I can't believe you'd want me to, after talking your ears off like that."

"I enjoy listening," she said.

"Can I have a peek?" Alex asked, gesturing to the paper.

She held it away from him. "When I'm finished, perhaps."

Alex laughed. "Okay, I won't try to see it. You know, you should really try to get Elise to pose for you. She's more suited to be a model than I am."

Lenora shook her head. "Beauty is not the goal of my work, Alex. I look for character in my subjects."

"Hey, she's got plenty of that, too," Alex said.

Lenora shook her head gently. "You are my model, Alex. One subject at a time is all I care to focus on."

"Whatever you say."

They walked inside together, a closeness in their bond that hadn't been there before. Alex was amazed by how at ease he'd felt sharing his feelings with a perfect stranger.

Elise was waiting by the front desk, the sign in her hands and a frown on her pursed lips.

"Alex, where have you been? Soon means less than an hour to me."

Alex said, "Sorry, we got carried away out on Bear Rocks."

Lenora said, "Thank you again, Alex. Until next time."

After she was gone, Elise said, "What did she mean by that?"

"It's nothing. She just wants me to pose again. So what's so urgent?"

Elise said, "You've got to do something about Mor and Emma. She called again while you were gone. Alex, she's frantic about the situation. She's afraid she's going to lose him if they don't patch this up soon."

"What can I do?" Alex asked. "I've talked to him once

and it didn't do any good at all. Besides, you know I hate to meddle."

"You care about your friends, don't you?"

"Elise, that's not fair. You know I do."

"Then we've got to do something, Alex."

He said, "I can talk to him again, but I can't imagine it will change his mind."

Elise said, "This calls for more than talk. We need to take some kind of action."

Alex thought about it a few moments, then said, "You're not going to stop pestering me until I do something, are you?"

Elise smiled grimly. "I like to think of it as being persistent."

"But you're not giving up," he pushed.

"No," she said firmly. "I believe in my heart that the two of them belong together."

Alex said, "It doesn't matter what either one of us thinks, it's how they feel that counts."

She started to rebut when he held up a hand. "Let me finish. If I promise to get them in the same room to give them a chance to talk this out, will you let me butt out if it doesn't work?"

She answered him with a brief hug. "I promise. Thanks, Alex."

After she pulled away, he said, "It's against my better judgment, but you're welcome."

He had an idea, but he still wasn't sure it was any of his business trying to get Emma and Mor back together.

At least if it didn't work, he'd be done with his "counselor" duties.

Alex knew it didn't take a genius to figure out how to get Mor out to Hatteras West. There was always something going wrong that needed the handyman's attention, though Alex prided himself on his own ability to fix a great many of the problems that popped up. Emma was an eager participant in the scheme, so she wouldn't have to be tricked into coming to the inn.

No, the real problem was bringing the two of them together without rousing Mor's suspicions that this was nothing more than a ploy to get them back together. And as much as Alex liked Emma, he didn't want to jeopardize his friendship with Mor. Losing him would be, in a very real sense, like losing a brother.

It had to be something big enough to get Mor's immediate attention, and yet not be too expensive to repair. After all, they were back on a tight budget at the Hatteras West Inn since the money from the emerald sale was finally gone.

With a sigh, Alex looked at his brand-new boiler, picked up a wrench to give it a rap, then realized he couldn't bring himself to do it. The lure was going to have to be something else.

Alex looked around the utility room, trying to spot a piece of nonessential equipment he could sabotage to get his friend out to the site in a hurry.

The fuse box would be the perfect diversion. Alex studied the penciled chart beside the box, found the fuse for the outside lights, then screwed the ancient round fuse out of the socket and substituted it with a blown fuse from the trash can near the door. He made it a point to substitute a smaller-amp fuse than needed. Mor would come out, spot the problem with the undersized fuse, and fix it, saving Alex an expensive bill he couldn't afford and giving Emma the chance to make peace.

After that, it was going to be in their hands.

He didn't want to play marriage counselor any more than he wanted to run for mayor.

15

Mor tossed the burnt fuse up and down in his hand and said, "What did you do, change this fuse in the dark? It's undersized, no wonder it kept blowing on you."

Alex had left it up to Elise to get Emma out to the inn, but the woman hadn't shown up yet, and to Alex's surprise, Mor had run right out. It looked as if his careful plan was about to fall apart.

Alex said, "Sorry I dragged you out for nothing. Do you have time for a game of backgammon before you go?"

Mor shook his head. "I'd love to, but with Les gone, it feels like I'm covering seven counties. I just happened to be over at Amy's shop working on one of her torches, that's the only reason you got me when you did. That timber-frame studio she had built is really sweet."

Amy Lang was Elkton Falls' local arts crowd unto herself, supporting herself with her sculptures, and taking welding jobs on the side when her cash ran low. She also happened to be one of Alex's closest neighbors, as the crow flew.

Well, he'd done his part in getting the split couple back

together. "Thanks for coming out," Alex said as he followed Mor to the equipment room door.

Emma was blocking the doorway, a stern look on her face. "Mor Pendleton, we need to talk."

"You've said enough lately, don't you think?" Mor asked. "Now step aside."

Emma was large enough to nearly fill the doorway, and if she was intent on staying there, Alex doubted Mor was willing to move her. She appeared to agree though, and Alex slipped past her. But before Mor could follow, she blocked the way again. "You I'm not done with."

"Woman, stand aside," Mor said, the edge hard in his voice.

"You don't intimidate me, you big bear. I'm not going anywhere until we talk this out."

Alex watched him from over Emma's shoulder and saw Mor's shoulders stiffen, then finally relax.

Mor said, "Of all the dumb, backward, half-cocked ideas I've ever heard in my life, your bone-headed stunt took the cake."

Emma said bravely, "Everybody has to be good at something."

Mor laughed gently. "You're a hard woman to stay mad at, you know that, don't you?"

Emma hugged him, her tears obvious in her voice. "Mor, don't you ever scare me like that again."

Alex backed away to give them some privacy and nearly stepped on Elise's foot. He had been so wrapped up in the reconciliation that he hadn't even noticed her approach.

She was smiling as a few tears tracked down her cheeks. "Now why are you crying?" he asked.

She shook her head. "Alex, sometimes you can be such a man."

"Thanks. I think," he added, still unsure whether it was a compliment or not.

Elise said, "Let's give them some privacy to finish patching things up."

"Okay by me, I didn't want to be their mediator in the first place."

She touched his shoulder lightly. "I don't know why, you're very good at it."

He grinned. "Okay then, I'm going to retire undefeated, one for one." He took a deep breath, then added, "Unless there's a chance you want to give me a shot at being two for two."

"How can I do that?" she asked.

"Well, there's another couple around here I'd really like to see get together," he said as earnestly as he could manage.

She just shook her head, but he could see a slight smile come to her lips before she turned away. At least he hadn't lost the knack for making her smile. It was something, anyway.

They worked at cleaning the lobby together, sweeping and dusting well after the last traces of lint were gone, waiting to see if their plan had worked. Twenty minutes later, Mor and Emma came out into the lobby holding hands.

Mor said, "If you two are still willing, the wedding's back on. Not only that, but we're moving it up."

Alex slapped him on the back. "Congratulations."

Elise hugged Emma and said, "I'm so happy for you both."

As the two women went into a whispered conversation regarding the on-again wedding plans, Mor said, "Wrong fuse, huh? You think you're pretty smart, don't you?"

"Hey, it was dark in there. Anybody can make a mistake."

Mor put one arm around Alex's shoulders and said, "Yeah, and you kept me from making a big one. Thanks."

"No problem. So I guess we're going to have that non–bachelor party after all."

"Looks like it," he said with a grin.

And at least one couple that belonged together was back on track.

Alex wished he'd been as successful with Elise, but seeing his best friend happy was enough.

It had to be; it looked like that was all Alex was going to get.

"This is it," Shantara told Alex as they loaded the last of his supplies into Alex's truck. "I'll let you know when those bulk soaps get in." Shantara gave Alex a huge price break on the disposables he needed to run the inn, with just a few conditions attached. Alex had to pick up the goods himself, something that was no hardship, since he usually welcomed an excuse to visit her at her general store. The only other condition was one night's stay a year at the inn in the Main Keeper's Suite, the one Mrs. Nesbitt was occupying now. Shantara usually picked a time when the inn was slow and she could afford a day and night away from the store. She'd picked January 28 for that year, a time when Alex had to fight to keep the budget above water.

Alex said, "Just give me a call and I'll pick the rest of my things up. How's Tracy holding up?"

Shantara frowned. "There are a thousand rumors flooding around the kudzu vine. Some folks are claiming she bumped Oxford off herself. I even heard somebody say they saw her around Mor's truck the day that stranger died. You want to know something, Alex? I think Conner's spreading them himself."

"I wouldn't put it past him," Alex said, "but I wouldn't worry about it too much either. Folks around here are too smart to fall for it."

Shantara raised one eyebrow at him. "Just like they were too smart to believe Finster's rumor about your lighthouse becoming an amusement park?"

A local Realtor, in an effort to get Alex to sell out, had started that rumor, along with a dozen others, and Alex well remembered how much grief the stories had caused him. "You've got a point, but I don't know what anybody can do about it."

"Tracy's offering to take a polygraph test, but the sheriff won't do it. He says he's got too much on his hands as it is, and he won't give in to the grandstanding."

Alex said, "He's got a point. Do me a favor, though. Don't start any rumors of your own, okay?"

She patted his cheek. "Alex, you're such a sweet man. Do us all a favor. Don't ever go into politics, okay? The sharks would eat you alive."

"You don't have to worry about me, I'm happy enough being an innkeeper."

As Alex stowed the last box on the back of his truck, he saw Grady Hatch across the street coming out of Buck's Grill.

"I need to talk to the mayor for a second, Shantara. Thanks again."

She smiled. "Glad to be of service, Alex. You don't have to restrict your visits to pickup days, you know that, don't you?"

"It's usually the only time Elise will let me out of the inn," Alex said with a laugh.

"How's that going?" she asked gently. "I heard about your big date."

"You and the rest of Elkton Falls. It didn't work out, that's all I've got to say about it." Before Shantara could ask for more details, Alex added, "I really do need to talk to Grady."

"You men, any excuse not to confide in someone else."

"Yeah, you're absolutely right, Shantara," he said as he rolled his eyes.

She was still laughing as Alex crossed the street.

He called out, "Mayor, do you have a second?"

Grady Hatch appeared to be deep in thought. It took two more hails from Alex before he realized he was being paged.

"Sorry about that, Alex, I was thinking about something else. Looks like Hurricane Zelda's coming ashore somewhere off the Outer Banks. I've got several friends out there, you know." The mayor usually spent his vacations on the coastal islands, claiming it was hard to believe he could drive eight hours and still be in North Carolina.

"I'm kind of partial to a particular landmark out there myself," Alex said with a smile.

"That's right, the other Hatteras Lighthouse is out that way. There's something else occupying my thoughts, though," the mayor said.

"Is the open road calling your name?" Alex asked lightly.

"Yep, that must be it. What can I do for you, Alex?"

Alex wasn't certain he wanted to talk about his concerns on Main Street. "Do you have a minute? You could walk me back to my truck."

Grady glanced at his watch, then said, "I've got just that. Is it important?"

Alex nodded, but held his tongue until they were back at his pickup. Somehow it seemed easier for men to talk with their feet on the back bumper of a pickup truck, their gaze locked ahead and not on each other.

Alex said, "I need to talk to you about Conner Shook."

The mayor said, "I'm keeping out of this election, Alex. I made a promise, and I'm sticking to it."

"That's what I want to talk to you about. I heard you had a pretty lively conversation with Conner the other day out my way."

The mayor's breath sharpened. "What did you hear?"

"Relax, Grady. I just hope you didn't agree to anything, since it sounded like Conner was pressuring you pretty hard."

Grady pulled his foot off the bumper and said, "You know what, Alex? That's one of the things I'm not going to miss about Elkton Falls. The compulsion this town has for knowing everybody else's business just isn't healthy."

"It's a part of living in a small town, you should know that better than anybody else. So is that what happened? Was Conner pushing you for an endorsement?"

The mayor nodded slowly. "I turned him down, just like I did the first dozen times he asked me. But the man's persistent, I've got to give him that."

"Don't give in, Grady. You don't want to be painted with the same brush as Conner just as you're leaving us.

Stay out of the election, just like you promised you would."

Grady looked sharply at him. "Is that a threat, Alex?"

He was honestly startled by the accusation. "Of course not. I just think we should all keep out of it and let the voters decide."

"That's what *I've* been trying to do," Grady said.

Alex admitted, "I haven't made it a secret that I'm backing Tracy, but then again, I don't have any pull around here."

Grady said, "Don't sell yourself short. Either one of them would be nervous if you ever decided to run against them."

Alex tried to laugh it off. "I've got something to run as it is, and Hatteras West takes every minute I've got."

Grady's expression softened. "Listen, I'm sorry I snapped at you. I just wish it were all over so I could start my retirement."

Alex said, "It won't be long now. The election's just around the corner."

"It can't get here fast enough for me, Alex." He glanced at his watch. "I'm really running behind, I need to scat."

"Stand firm, Grady," Alex said as the mayor rushed off.

Grady Hatch stuck one thumb up in the air as he hurried away. Alex considered telling Shantara what Conner was up to, but truly, there was nothing any of them could do about it if Grady caved in at the last minute and gave Conner his endorsement. The only purpose it would serve would be to put Tracy under even more stress than she already was.

No, that was one item of gossip he was going to keep to himself.

Alex was pulling out when Shantara flagged him down.

He put the truck in park and rolled down his window. "What's up, did that soap come in while I was gone?"

She waved a sheet of paper at him, folded neatly in half. "Not hardly. This fax just came in for a couple staying out at the inn, the Joneses. I was told to keep it here for them to pick up, but since you're heading back out that way, it will save them a trip." Shantara's General Store was so much more than just a mercantile. She had a post office in one corner, sold crafts in another, and had just opened a copy center/office services feature in a back storeroom that had long ago held cattle and pig feed.

"I'll be glad to take it to them," he said as he took the sheet and put it on the pile of junk that rested between the two passenger spots on the bench seat.

Just his luck, Alex got stuck behind a tractor going ten miles an hour on his way back to the inn. The farm equipment wasn't strictly street legal, but nobody ever complained. Small-town farmers around Elkton Falls were in enough trouble as it was without being hassled by the law or its citizenry. Alex did his best to buy his produce from them whenever he could. He recognized Hank Wilkins, one of Irene's nephews, driving the tractor in front of him. The criminologist/cosmetologist had more family than Adam around Elkton Falls, and she made no secret of the fact that Hank was one of her favorites.

Alex waved to the beefy man, who was lost in his own thoughts as he chugged slowly up the road.

He wasn't prying, and spying had never been his intent, but Alex found his gaze wandering to the fax the Joneses had received, more out of boredom and curiosity than anything else.

A breeze blew into the truck, and the folded paper blew open. Alex only got a quick glance at the printing inside, but it was enough.

He nearly wrecked when he saw the letterhead printed across the top.

It was from *The Tattle Tale,* the tabloid he'd seen marked up in their "honeymoon" suite, and from the look of things, it could only mean one thing: trouble.

The rest of the drive back, he kept fighting himself whether to read the entire fax or not. After all, it was private, just like someone's mail, and he'd never peeked at any of his guests' mail since he'd become an innkeeper.

But was it, really? A fax was more open, more public. So why would they be getting a letter from a sensational tabloid magazine?

He was still mulling over what to do by the time he got to the inn.

Elise heard him drive up and met him at the back door near their storeroom. She smiled gently. "That didn't take long. Usually you stretch your trips into town a lot longer than that."

He said, "I didn't want to leave you stranded too long without backup. Elise, I need some advice."

Certainly she was a pretty woman, but there was a lot more to Elise than looks. Alex respected her opinion and her judgment, had in fact deferred to her on more than a few occasions.

"I'll do what I can."

Alex tapped the paper in his hand. "This came for the Joneses, our newlyweds. It's a fax from Shantara's store."

"What about it?" she asked, looking at the paper as she spoke.

How could he phrase this without making himself look bad? Taking a deep breath, Alex said, "As I was driving back to the inn, the page flew open, and purely by accident, I saw the letterhead. It's something I'm having a hard time figuring."

"You didn't read it, did you, Alex?"

"Come on, give me some credit."

She looked at him intently, waiting for him to go on.

He said, "Hey, I'm not saying I wasn't tempted to scan it, but I didn't. The only problem is, there might be trouble. The letterhead said—"

Elise held up a hand. "Don't tell me, I don't want to know. Alex, our guests have a right to their privacy. I shouldn't have to lecture you about that, not after we both lost our master keys."

"This is completely different," Alex said.

"How do you see that?"

"Elise, if they wanted it to be that private, they wouldn't have sent it as a fax." The couple had grumbled about the lack of private phone plug-ins for their computers after they'd checked in, but that was a service Alex didn't offer. Rewiring the inn, with its ancient walls of lath and plaster, just wasn't in his budget, nor would he do it even if he owned his own emerald mine. He liked running an old-fashioned inn. In his mind, Hatteras West was a place to get away from all that.

Alex added, "I'm sure Shantara didn't think twice about it, but something in here could adversely affect the inn."

Elise thought about it a moment, then held out her hand. "I suppose there's only one way to know for sure. Let me see it."

16

Alex held the paper away from her. "I don't want you to compromise your principles on my account."

She said, "No you don't. You dragged me into this, and now I don't see any way around it."

He nodded, started to hand it to her, then thought better of it and opened the paper himself. Elise was startled by the letterhead from *The Tattle Tale* as she read over his shoulder, but both of them nearly yelped when they saw the body of the message.

It said:

> *Okay, if you can't get a picture of the room, fake something. We need "The Murder Inn" story by Friday, and I want art to go with it. Here's my authorization; bribe the maid if you can't steal the key again, but I want a picture of that room to go along with the story, or don't bother coming back.*

It was signed, "Jasper Hayes, Editor-in-Chief, *The Tattle Tale*."

"So that's what happened to our keys," Elise said, fuming. "I want them gone, Alex. We don't need their money that badly."

A sudden idea struck him. "If they go now, they'll just write the story anyway. Maybe there's a way to kill it altogether."

"How are we going to do that?" she asked.

"I've got an idea, but I'm going to need help from you." She smiled grimly. "Count me in."

And suddenly, the two of them were joined in a conspiracy of their own.

Alex's alarm screamed at 2:00 A.M. He reached groggily for the snooze button, then remembered why he'd set it for such a miserable hour.

It was time to put all their hard work into play. Dressing quickly in black sweatpants and a navy blue sweatshirt, Alex pulled a ski mask over his face and headed out into the lobby.

Elise was waiting for him by the front desk.

"You look like you're going to rob a bank," she said with a smile.

Alex pulled off the mask and asked, "Are you ready?"

Elise said, "I don't know about this, Alex. I'm having second thoughts. It feels so juvenile."

"Come on, they deserve it. If you don't want to be a part of it, I understand, but I'm going through with my end of it."

Elise said, "Then I'm not going to let you have all the fun."

Alex looked at his watch. "Okay, give me five minutes to get set up, then start the tape."

She said, "I'm glad you got these walkie-talkies from Mor. I can't wait to hear what they say."

Mor had loaned Alex three walkie-talkies he'd repaired for a trio of brothers who used them during hunting season. Earlier that day, Alex had slipped one into the newlyweds' room behind the dresser. It would let them eavesdrop on the effects of their work.

Alex said, "Here goes nothing."

He went up to the second floor and used the attic scuttle in the maid's closet to get into the attic. Alex had traded in his normal high-powered flashlight for one of considerably less intensity. It was enough light to let him see by, but not enough to broadcast his presence to the world in case someone happened to glance up at the single window in the attic space.

Grabbing a bamboo pole he used to knock hornets' nests down in the autumn, Alex climbed out onto the roof until he was even with the reporters' suite. Leaning outward near the gutter, Alex was ready to begin.

A quick glance at his watch showed that it was nearly time.

With a soft, delicate touch, Alex lowered the pole and tapped it gently on the second-floor window. He pulled the pole up, waited ten breaths, then tapped again, this time with more vigor than before. Jerking the pole back toward him, Alex almost lost his balance and fell.

How would he explain what had happened if he slipped from his perch? The best he could hope for from a fall at that height would be a broken bone or two, and he didn't even want to think about the worst possibility.

Alex hit the broadcast button and signaled to Elise. The system was sophisticated enough to allow them to monitor the broadcasts from each other while only receiving from the third set, so their conversations wouldn't be sent at an inopportune time to the room they were trying to haunt."

Alex asked, "Any reaction at all?"

"They heard you, they've been fighting about it. The light's been on for five minutes. Hang on. Okay, they just turned it out again. Give it a few minutes, then hit it again."

From her spot in the maid's closet, Elise could watch their door without being in their line of sight if they came out suddenly.

Alex waited, staring up at the lighthouse. He was in clear view of the observation platform, but it was closed for the night. What would the sentinel think of his foolishness? Alex had to admit, the lighthouse had seen him do a lot worse, though not lately. With a grin, he saluted the tower with his free hand.

It was time for another tap.

After a quick rapping, he pulled up the pole just in time to hear the window slam upward.

Alex didn't need Elise's monitoring to hear the voices inside.

"What was it, a tree branch?" Sheila asked.

Paul said, "There's nothing out here, I keep telling you that."

"That wasn't nothing," she hissed loudly. "Tell me you didn't hear it."

"So I heard something. It was probably just the wind."

She said, "The wind doesn't knock on your window, you idiot."

"Well, there's nobody out there. We're two stories up. Do you honestly think somebody's up on stilts trying to get our attention?"

She said loudly, "Close that window. You're letting in a draft."

Good. They were unsettled enough for the moment. Alex carefully climbed back to the window and slipped inside. Elise was waiting for him there, having climbed up the scuttle herself.

"You've really got them going," she said.

"I know, I heard. Are we ready for phase II?"

She held up a set of chains he used in winter. "All set."

"Okay, here goes."

Alex started moaning loudly as Elise walked in increasingly large circles away from him, dragging the chains on the rough pine floor of the attic as she added her own set of groans to Alex's mix. They were hoping the sounds were split enough to make the pair just below think there were several ghosts above them. Mrs. Nesbitt had warned them early on that she could sleep through a hurricane, and the other rooms in that section were empty, so they didn't have to worry about disturbing anyone else with their antics. That was the only way Elise had agreed to the charade.

It was hard not to laugh, and a few of Alex's groans sounded distinctly like snickers. Maybe they'd think one of the ghosts was insane!

Finally, they were ready for their crowning touch. Alex motioned to Elise, gestured to the window again, and climbed back out onto the roof. Elise's job would be to whisper into the microphone, "Leave us, leave us, leave us," as Alex tapped on the window again.

Alex got to his previous spot, leaned over, and started to tap as he lost his balance again. The bamboo pole slipped from his hand as he went over, sending his foot through the window! The glass shattered as Alex caught himself and pulled back up on the gutter. That had been entirely too close.

Alex scrambled back inside, glad he'd worn his work boots instead of his flimsy running shoes. His little stunt could have ended in disaster in a dozen different ways.

Elise's eyes were bright in the weak light. "What happened?"

"I slipped and nearly fell. My foot went through the window as it was."

"Alex, are you all right?"

"I am now, but I think I've haunted my last room. I hope the glass didn't hit them."

They turned on the walkie-talkie and listened to the room below.

Paul said frantically, "I don't care about the story anymore. I'm getting out of here."

"You're not leaving me behind," Sheila yelled.

"Hey, you're on your own. If you're not ready in two minutes, I'm out of here, with or without you. Pretending to be married to you was just about more than I could take. I'm not about to hang around here and let a ghost get me. If you want to write the story, be my guest, but I'm not touching it."

"You wouldn't dare leave me here alone," she screeched.

"Just watch me."

Alex tried to fight the laughter bubbling in his throat, but a few sounds still escaped before he could get himself back under control.

Sheila snapped, "Did you hear that? They're coming back."

"I'm going. Now," Paul shouted loudly enough for them to hear without the aid of the walkie-talkies.

"Wait for me. I'm coming, too," Sheila screamed.

Alex and Elise waited a few minutes at the window, then watched the two of them hurrying out to their car in the parking lot, trailing errant articles of clothing along the way.

Elise said, "Oh, Alex, we shouldn't have."

He shrugged. "Now if they write about hauntings at the Murder Inn, they can draw from their own experiences."

As he started down the scuttle, she said, "What do we do now?"

"You go back to bed. I've got to get a piece of cardboard and patch that window until I can fix it in the morning."

He'd half hoped Elise would offer to help, but she stifled a yawn and said, "See you in few hours then."

He was at the door when Mrs. Nesbitt came out of her room. "Alex Winston, what in the world is going on around here?"

"Sorry," he said sheepishly. "We had a little trouble, but it's all been taken care of now. I thought you were a heavy sleeper."

"I am, but that ruckus could have wakened the dead." She looked at the room where the reporters had been staying. "Were they the cause of it?"

"Indirectly. Don't worry, they just checked out."

She nodded her approval. "Good riddance. You want to know something? They weren't lighthouse fans at all."

"It takes all kinds," Alex said.

After Mrs. Nesbitt retired, Alex swept up the broken glass inside the Joneses' room, relishing how much fun it had been doing something active to deal with that particular problem.

Patching the hole, he regretted not being able to do anything more constructive to help Emma, Mor, and Tracy with their problems.

There were some things a good haunting just couldn't fix.

"I wonder if this rain is going to keep people from voting," Alex asked as he looked out the front windows of the inn the next morning. It was pouring outside, a steady rain that had started at dawn and seemed to intensify with each passing hour.

Elise said, "What I'm wondering about is which candidate it will hurt the most."

Alex leaned against the desk. "I've got a feeling every vote's going to count in this election. I'm going to go myself right after lunch."

"I'd like to go with you, if you don't mind."

Alex smiled. "I didn't realize you'd registered here. I'd love to have you go with me. That's why we have signs for the desk. We should have the rooms finished by then, now that things are slowing down."

Elise said, "Don't worry, Alex, business will pick back up."

"Maybe we shouldn't have run the Jones twosome off. Any publicity would be better than what we're getting now."

"Think about it. Do you really want the inn full of the kind of people who read *The Tattle Tale*?"

He smiled. "I've got a feeling the nightly hauntings would get a little old after a while."

"So let's be happy with the guests we have. I need some time off later after we vote. Emma and I have a few last-minute arrangements to make for the wedding."

"What do you need besides a minister and a marriage license?"

She shook her head. "You're kidding, right? Irma

Bean's doing the reception; she's even taking care of the wedding cake. We've got the Mountain Express performing at the reception, you should approve of them since they play a lot of bluegrass, and Shantara's helping us line up our wait staff. This is going to be some celebration."

Alex said, "It would be even better if we knew for sure what really happened to Toby Sturbridge. I'm pretty sure Sheriff Armstrong isn't too optimistic about finding the killer now, though he won't admit it. I think he's losing interest since he's been trying to figure out who killed Oxford Hitchcock. A local victim's bound to get priority over a stranger nobody around Elkton Falls is going to miss."

"As long as he gives up on the idea that Mor or Emma had anything to do with her ex-husband's death, I don't care. The thought of that man even being on the grounds still gives me the shivers."

Alex said, "I hate the fact he terrorized Emma as much as you do, but he still didn't deserve what he got."

Elise was about to say something else when Lenora walked in.

Elise said, "I'll talk to you later. I've got to get started on those rooms."

After she was gone, Lenora said, "I hope she didn't leave on my account."

"We've got a busy morning ahead of us if we're going to vote in the election today."

Lenora smiled softly. "So, are you voting for green or red?"

"I'm not voting by color. The entire town's gone crazy with red and green, gold and blue. I've been supporting Tracy since I first found out she was running for mayor. I just hope she wins. Is there something I can do for you?"

"Alex, I'm afraid it's nearing the time for me to move on. I plan to check out tomorrow, and I was wondering if you'd have time to pose for me one last time today."

He scratched his head as he studied the register. "I'd love to help, but I've got my hands full the next twenty-four hours."

She nodded. "I understand. Perhaps I could follow you

around as you work this morning and get a few quick sketches while you clean."

"You're a hard lady to say no to, aren't you?"

She shrugged. "I don't mean to be so persistent, but it's important to me."

Alex was about to decline, then surprised himself by agreeing to her idea. "If you can't think of a better way to spend the morning, you're welcome to tag along with me."

She smiled brightly. "Wonderful. When do we get started?"

"Now's as good a time as any. We'll do your room first."

All morning long, Lenora followed Alex around, talking little but sketching furiously. She was filling up sheet after sheet on her pad, focusing on him as he cleaned floors, scoured bathrooms, made beds, and dusted furniture.

He said, "Am I going to be able to see these before you go?"

"Perhaps I'll share one of them with you. We'll see."

Elise knocked on the door later when he was working and said, "Alex, I need more . . ." Her words died as she spotted Lenora in the room with him. "Sorry, I didn't know you were with someone."

"She's shadowing me today," Alex said.

"I won't interrupt, then," Elise said.

Lenora looked up from her sketch pad and said, "Please go about your business, you won't disturb me."

With Elise's gaze still on Lenora, she said, "I need more window cleaner and we're out in the supply closet."

Alex went to his cart and handed her his bottle. "This is my last room and I'm just about finished. I'll get more from Shantara later."

Elise merely nodded as she accepted the cleaner, carefully avoiding eye contact with either one of them as she left.

Now what was that all about, Alex wondered.

He tucked the last corner of the blanket in on the bed

and said, "That's it. You've got to be tired of sketching me by now. You must have drawn a dozen pictures today."

Lenora closed the pad and held it close to her. "I could draw you for a week, Alex. There's something about you, something deep and clear that I can't seem to capture. I wish you could pose for me in my studio."

"Where's that?" Alex asked.

"Paris," she answered simply.

"Unless you're talking about Paris, Kentucky, there's not much chance of that. I don't do much traveling in Europe." Truth be told, Alex had never been west of the Mississippi, let alone outside the United States. Being an innkeeper held two major drawbacks for travel; not enough time or money.

"A pity, that," she said. "I'd like to give you something for your trouble."

Alex smiled. "I'd never admit it to anyone else, but I kind of enjoyed it."

"Still, you deserve something," Lenora said.

"Draw something for me, then," he said, joking.

Lenora merely nodded. "Thank you again, Alex."

He found Elise downstairs waiting on him. She said, "Where's your shadow?"

"She's finished with me," Alex said.

Elise replied, "If you say so."

Alex said, "I've got an idea. Why don't we grab lunch at Buck's after we vote?"

There was a hesitation to Elise's reply, and Alex added, "We can go Dutch if you'd like."

Elise shook her head. "No, I'd be delighted to join you for lunch as your guest."

It wasn't exactly the second date he'd been hoping for, but at least it was something.

17

"I can't believe the polls are this crowded for a local election," Elise said as she and Alex waited in line to vote at Elkton Falls Elementary School.

"Don't forget, this is one of the highlights of the social season," Alex said with a smile. "It's a perfect excuse for everyone to get together."

Up ahead of the long snaking line, Alex saw Conner on one side of the entry to the gymnasium, with Tracy right across from him. They were handing out badges, buttons, pencils, and flyers to any voter who would take them. Elkton Falls was pretty strict about letting their candidates roam around. It was a good rule, Alex thought, brought on by the year Lester Ferngate accosted nearly everyone in sight when he was trying to unseat Grady Hatch.

Grady himself was walking down the line, stopping for a word now and then and shaking a lot of hands. When he got to Alex, he faltered a step, then said, "Glad you folks could make it out. I just have one question. If you two are here, who's watching the inn?"

Alex said, "We thought they'd be able to manage on their own long enough for us to vote."

Elise asked, "So how does it feel with your final term as mayor winding down?"

Grady said, "You want to know the truth? I thought I'd enjoy it more without the pressure of trying to get elected, but it's taken some of the zip out of it, I can tell you that."

Elise smiled. "You can always run again in two years."

He laughed at that. "No, Ma'am, my days of public service are over. It's hard to say where I'll be two years from now."

Alex asked, "Is everything all right?"

Grady slapped him on the shoulder. "Everything's just fine, Alex. All is well."

As the mayor moved on, Elise said, "He seems preoccupied, doesn't he?"

Alex could have shared with her the talk he'd had with the mayor, but he decided not to. "He's most likely got a lot on his mind."

Smiley O'Reilly came out of the polling booth with a flag sticker on his lapel. Smiley had a habit of dropping the first few words of every sentence he spoke, which could get confusing when he was pitching some of the insurance he sold.

He stopped by them and said, "Folks. Old truck still running, Alex?" The twinkle in his eye was bright.

"Better than yours," Alex said with a chuckle.

Smiley rolled his eyes, tipped his cap to Elise, and said, "Ma'am."

After he was gone, Elise said, "I love this town. Where else are you going to meet such interesting people?"

"We're unusual, but I'm not sure I'd go as far as saying we're all that interesting."

She said, "Oh, but you are."

As they approached the two candidates' positions, Conner struck first. "Any chance you've changed your mind, Alex?"

He replied, "No, I'm voting for Tracy."

Conner still smiled brightly. "Have a pencil anyway. I've got a ton of them."

Alex just shook his head, and Conner moved on to

Elise. "How about you, fair lady, do you have any interest in a badge? I'd be glad to pin it on for you."

She smiled and said, "No, thanks. I just wouldn't feel right taking it, seeing that I'll be voting for your ex-wife."

Conner laughed. "Man, this is a tough crowd."

A young woman behind them said, "I'd love a badge," and Conner turned his charm on her.

Alex said to Tracy, "He hasn't changed a bit, has he?"

"No, that's always been one of his problems. He still thinks this is for junior class president."

Elise asked, "How is it going so far?"

"I think the town's pretty evenly split, if the way folks are acting is any indication. It's too close to call, that's for sure."

Alex said, "I'm just glad those newspaper photographs didn't hurt you."

She smiled gently. "Hurt me? If anything, they gave me a higher profile than I had before. I've had several folks tell me how rotten I was treated by the press, and a few even said they changed their votes for me after seeing the way they behaved."

Alex shook his head. "Somebody should teach them some manners. We are still in the South."

Tracy said, "You'll have to get in line. I think it's absolutely hilarious it all backfired on them."

Elise touched Tracy's arm. "Good luck. I'm voting for you."

She smiled at that. "Thanks, Elise. Now I know I've got at least two in my favor."

Alex protested, "Hey, I'm voting for you, too."

She said, "Watch out, folks, it could be a landslide."

Finally the line moved into the gymnasium itself. Mrs. Hurley was at the Voter's Registration table, the big leather-bound book open in front of her. Irma Bean, standing right beside her, said, "State your name and address," to Alex.

"Alex Winston, the Hatteras West Inn. That's on Point Road, if you're not sure."

Irma wrinkled her nose. "Alex, no foolishness from you, we have to do this by the book."

Mrs. Hurley said, "Irma, I know more of these folks than you do. I had Alex in my grade school class in this very building."

"Now Dot, you know what the book says."

Mrs. Hurley smiled gently. "And if I should forget, you're right here to remind me, aren't you?"

Irma flushed slightly as she handed Alex a ballot. "Next," she said as she winked at Elise.

"Elise Danton, also of Hatteras West," she said.

Mrs. Hurley scanned the book, then said, "Sorry, I don't have you listed here."

Elise was crestfallen. "I'm not on the rolls? But I registered three months ago."

Mrs. Hurley said, "Don't worry, dear, if you're in here, I'll find you." She riffled through the pages, then said, "Here you are. Grianna Monk put you down with the *E*'s instead of the *D*'s. What was that woman thinking?"

"Most likely she was still mooning over Silas Lake. Seems to me three months ago the two of them were hot and heavy. Old Grianna could barely spell her own name back then, let alone somebody else's."

"May I still vote?" Elise asked.

Irma said, "Absolutely. Here's your ballot. Pick up a pen at the table over there, and don't forget to put it back when you're done."

Mrs. Hurley added, "She can't be done, she's not a roast, Irma. But she can be finished with her ballot."

Irma rolled her eyes. "That's what I get for volunteering with a retired schoolteacher."

Alex walked to one of the curtained booths and checked off Tracy's name on the ballot. He found Elise waiting for him. "One thing about the Elkton Falls Election Ballot, you don't waste a lot of time pondering."

Irma said sharply, "Hold it down, please, folks are trying to vote."

Alex waved a hand, then put his ballot in the welded steel box that sat by itself on a long maple table. Amy had cobbled the ballot box up in her shop a few years ago after the last ancient wooden receptacle had finally fallen apart.

This monstrosity would outlast them all, and it took three boys from the high school football team to carry it over to the town hall for the tabulating.

After they were back outside, Elise said, "Is that all there is to it?"

"Anticlimactic, isn't it? Tell you what. Why don't we go over to Buck's and grab that lunch I promised you."

"I thought you'd never ask," she said.

Buck's was crowded with voters escaping the rain, and Alex wondered briefly if any work was getting done in town at all that day except by Buck and Sally Anne.

Sandra was at a booth and waved them over. "I'm just leaving, if you'all would like a place to sit."

"Thanks," Alex said as he slid in after her. "Have you heard anything else about Toby Sturbridge or Oxford Hitchcock?"

Sandra counted out a few bills, then said, "No, it's been quiet on both fronts. Our good sheriff appears to be baffled at this point." She put her money on the table, then said, "I've got to run, I'm late for an appointment with a new client. Alex, your uncle Jase would have shot me for working on Election Day, but since he passed away, I don't seem to get any time off at all. It was good seeing you two."

Sally Anne hurried over and bussed their table. "Sorry about that. Things have been crazy all day." She added softly to Alex, "We need to talk later."

Alex nodded. "Call me at the inn. I'll be back there in an hour or two. Unless it's urgent," he added.

"No, it can wait that long. Now what can I get you two?"

After they'd ordered, it wasn't three minutes before Sheriff Armstrong came in. He waved to a few of the folks present, then ambled over to Alex and Elise. "What brings you two into town with an inn full of people?"

"We're not that full at the moment. Besides, we came in to vote," Elise said. "Have you cast your ballot yet?"

Armstrong said, "First thing this morning. It was a real privilege to see a ballot without my name on it." Since the sheriff's elections had been switched to every other year opposite the mayoral elections, the sheriff was enjoying the second year of a unique three-year term.

Alex had wanted some time alone with Elise, but having the sheriff at their table was too good an opportunity to pass up. "Care to join us?" he asked. "We just got here."

"No, sir, I've already eaten, but thanks for asking."

Alex said, "Then let's just cut to the chase. Have there been any developments you can talk about?"

Armstrong said loudly, "We've got a list of suspects we're looking closely at right now. I expect an arrest to be made any day now."

Alex said, "Okay, you've made your public service announcement to the crowd. Now what's the truth?"

Armstrong said in a near-whisper, "I'm no closer to finding the killers than I was the day each man died. Truth be told, I'm beginning to wonder if I shouldn't bring the state troopers in on both these cases. Blast it all, I'm still the sheriff, I want to do it myself. I'll get them, don't you worry about that."

As Armstrong moved to another table, Alex said, "I'm sorry I invited him without asking you first, but I had to know about his progress."

Elise said, "I don't mind. I was surprised, though, to hear you invite someone else out on our date."

Alex laughed. "Oh, no, I'm not making that mistake again, labeling something a date. It puts entirely too much pressure on both of us."

She said, "I suppose so," then studied her menu.

After they ordered, Elise said, "I've been wondering about something, Alex. Do you think there's a chance the same person killed Toby Sturbridge and Oxford Hitchcock? It's hard to imagine two murderers roaming around Elkton Falls at the same time."

Alex said, "I kind of doubt they're related. To be honest with you, I wonder if the person who killed Toby even realized it at the time. That had to be an accident. Who would ever suspect a blow to the chest could kill a man?

Oxford, on the other hand, took a board to the head. There was nothing accidental about that."

"It just seems like a coincidence that both men died so close together."

Alex nodded. "It was a run of bad luck for Elkton Falls, no doubt about that, but murders happen in small towns, too. Sometimes I think they're more noticeable than the homicide statistics in the big cities."

Sally Anne brought them their plates, and Alex noticed there was a folded note under his. Sneaking it out, he glanced down at his lap and read it.

DON'T CALL ME. I'LL COME OUT TO THE INN LATER.

Alex looked up to find Elise studying him. "Is it in code, or can you read it without your decoder ring?"

Alex handed her the note under the table. After she read it, Elise said, "I think Sally Anne's enjoying her little spying venture with you."

"I think you're right." He took a bite of his club sandwich and added, "She's in the perfect place to hear things, though. I wonder what she's got to say."

Elise said, "I couldn't even begin to guess."

After they finished, Alex said, "Okay, one more stop at Shantara's to restock our glass cleaner and we can head back to the inn."

"If somebody hasn't walked off with it by now," Elise said with a smile.

"Hey, the only time I had that problem was when we had the Golden Days Fair out there, and I'm never going through that again."

"Are you forgetting Sarah March? I still can't believe what she did."

A few months before, one of their guests, a woman named Sarah March, had taken every lightbulb from her room upon checking out. It had taken Alex a second to realize they were really gone when he switched on her lights and nothing had happened.

He said, "Okay, maybe we'd better head on back."

Elise said, "Oh, Alex, I'm just teasing. We have time to pick up the cleaner."

Once he was parked in front of Shantara's store, Alex said, "Are you coming in?"

Elise said, "If you don't mind, I'd like to stay out here and enjoy some of this sunshine." The rain had finally stopped, and the sun was out in all its glory, giving everything wet a special sheen of brilliance.

He said, "Good enough. I'll be back in a minute."

Shantara looked up from her clearance table as Alex walked in and said, "What are you doing here two days in a row? People are going to talk. Besides, I thought you had guests to take care of."

Alex said, "I'm glad everyone's so concerned about my inn. I need some glass cleaner."

She pointed him in the general direction, then moved over to the window and looked out. "Have you voted yet?"

"Elise and I struck our blows for democracy, and then we ate at Buck's. Don't worry, we voted for your candidate."

Shantara waved to Elise in the truck, then said, "Why didn't she come in?"

"She's getting a little fresh air," Alex said.

Shantara asked, "You two seem to be getting along better, aren't you?"

"When we're not trying to go out on dates, we're completely compatible," he said with a shrug.

"So don't date her again. You can still take the girl out to dinner now and then, and if there happens to be a good night kiss or two thrown into the mix, what's the harm in that?"

"When you're done matchmaking, add these to my bill," Alex said as he held up two bottles of cleaner. "These should hold me until my order comes in."

Shantara said, "I'll give you a call. Think about what I said, Alex."

"I'm sorry, were you talking to me?" he asked with a smile.

Alex ducked just as a bath sponge from the discount table sailed over his head.

18

"Have you heard the news?" Sally Anne asked Alex that evening as she brought by her delivery.

"No, I've been waiting for you. I must confess, your note has me curious," Alex said. Ever since Sally Anne had passed him her message at the diner, Alex had been wondering what she had to share.

"Not that, this is huge, and hot info. They can't come up with a winner."

"How's that possible?" Alex asked. "There weren't any hanging chads or other ballot problems like Florida had a while back."

Sally Anne said, "Don't kid yourself. We got a call from the Board of Elections for soup and sandwiches, and I talked Dad into letting me deliver them to the courthouse. From what I heard over there, they kept coming up with different totals. Tracy won by three votes one time, and Conner won by two the next. They'll probably be there all night."

"I knew it was going to be close, but I can't believe they're having so much trouble with a handful of ballots."

Sally Anne said, "You should have heard them arguing

over some of the votes. One woman checked off both candidates, then wrote her own name in the write-in spot. They threw that one out, but there were some with smudges that a couple of folks wanted to disqualify, and I don't know what else was happening. They threw me out before I had the chance to hear anything else."

"Tracy must be going crazy," Alex said as he stored the muffins and pastries next to the breakfast bar. "So what was your other news?"

Sally Anne said, "I overheard at the diner that Conner and Mayor Hatch were out this way together a couple of days ago, and they weren't too happy with each other."

Alex didn't have the heart to tell her that he'd already heard that himself from Lenora. "He was probably pushing for an endorsement."

"Well, from what I saw, he didn't get it." Sally Anne added, "I'd better run. I want to be back at the grill in case the board needs anything else. This is the most excitement we've had around here in a while."

Alex almost added, "If you don't count murder," but he kept that to himself. There was nothing to be gained by bringing the waitress back to the reality of homicide.

The next morning, Lenora checked out before Alex even had the chance to put the buffet out.

"I'm going to be sorry to see you go," Alex said as he filled out her credit card slip.

"I can never stay in one place too long. I become attached, and it becomes harder and harder to leave. Alex, I want to thank you for your cooperation in modeling for me."

"I was glad to do it." He lowered his voice so Elise wouldn't hear his next words. "I'm going to miss our conversations. I truly enjoyed talking to you."

She leaned forward and kissed him on the cheek. "The pleasure was mine as well."

Alex looked up in time to see Elise look away. There was nothing he could do about that now.

"Let me help you with your bags," Alex said as he handed her the receipt from her bill.

"That would be greatly appreciated," she said.

As Alex followed her out the front door, he called to Elise, "I'll be right back."

"Take your time. I've got this covered." There was a definite touch of frost in her voice.

Outside, Lenora said, "I'm sorry if I've caused any difficulties between you and Elise."

Alex laughed softly. "Any difficulties were there long before you got here." He handed her one of her sketch pads and said, "Hey, I never got to see these."

She took them from him and said, "Good things come to he who waits."

After her luggage and pads were stowed safely away, Lenora said, "Remember what I said, Alex. Have patience in all things."

He said, "That's not one of my strong points."

She touched his cheek lightly with her hand, then said, "It is a trait worth cultivating."

After she was gone, Alex headed back inside. Elise met him at the door and said, "We're running low on guests again, aren't we?"

Alex nodded. "I had three cancellations because of the pending hurricane. Nobody wants to travel right now, even if we're nowhere near its path. I heard on the news last night that it could come inland as soon as tonight."

Elise said, "I'm just glad we're far enough in not to worry about it, though a rainstorm could ruin the wedding tomorrow night."

Alex said, "Are you kidding? I don't think Mother Nature herself wants to mess with Emma Sturbridge on her wedding day."

"Are you and Mor still intent on having a bachelor party tonight?"

Alex said, "It's almost a crime to call it that, but yes, Mor and Les and I are having it out here tonight. Les just got back into town, sporting a suntan and a peeling red nose. How about Emma? What's she going to do while we're chewing over old times?"

Elise said, "We're going to be at her cottage this evening working on the birdseed throwaways instead of rice. That should keep us busy until late."

Alex nodded. "The guys are coming out here around seven, and I can't imagine it lasting past ten. Since Mor's staying out here tonight, I'm putting him in Number 7 as soon as I get it cleaned up."

That was Lenora's room. "She was an interesting woman, wasn't she?" Elise asked.

"Once I got over the shock of being her model, I really got to like her. She was pretty closemouthed about what she was sketching, though. I asked her half a dozen times to let me see her work, but she always turned me down."

Elise said, "You know how artists can be about their creations." She paused, then said, "I've got a light load this morning. Why don't I help you clean your rooms today?"

"That sounds great. To be honest with you, I'd be glad for your company. I've missed working side by side with you."

She nodded. "Good. Let's do it then."

When they got to Number 7, Alex and Elise were surprised to find something taped to the mirror.

It was a charcoal sketch of Alex, with the lighthouse in the background.

Elise studied it, then said, "She really is quite good, isn't she?"

Alex replied, "That's the first thing of hers I've seen. The whole time she was drawing me, I wasn't allowed to even peek."

Elise studied the drawing another full minute, then said, "You've really got to have this framed."

"Why would anybody want to have a drawing of me on their wall?"

"I think it's perfect for the lobby, Alex. If you won't frame it yourself, I'll have Mor do it."

Alex shook his head. "That's all I need, my best friend

thinking I've lost my mind plastering the inn with my own picture."

"Well, someone needs to frame it."

Alex reluctantly said, "If you really think it belongs here, I'll do it myself."

Elise found a folded note on the dresser and handed it to Alex. "Here, this is for you, too."

He opened it and read aloud, "A small gift for all you've given me. Lenora."

Elise said, "Well, she was certainly fond of you."

"It's the inn. You know how it affects some people that way."

After they finished cleaning the room, Elise carefully removed the tape holding the sketch and carried it gingerly to her room. Alex wasn't sure how he felt about having his own portrait hanging in the lobby, but from the look in Elise's eyes, he knew it was useless to argue.

Soon enough it would be just one more part of Hatteras West, blending in with everything else, a hodgepodge that had somehow become a tapestry of his heritage.

Lenora had made sure that she'd always be a part of the inn.

Mor and Les came out to Hatteras West together a little before seven. Since Emma didn't believe in wedding rehearsals, there was no need for a rehearsal dinner, freeing Mor the night before the wedding. Les, grinning broadly by his side, had a six-pack of beer in one hand and a bottle of champagne in the other.

"Wow, you broke out the good stuff," Alex said.

Les said, "I swore to myself on the day we became partners that if this hound dog ever settled down, I'd give him a bon voyage. So where should we have this little party?"

Alex said, "Mor, it's your call. The place is just about empty, so wherever you want is fine."

"How about the top of the lighthouse?" he asked with a grin.

Les said, "You know, I haven't been up there in donkey years. Lead on."

Mor looked startled. "I was only half-kidding. I'm not sure those steps and your alcohol are the best combination."

Les said, "Come on, man, where's your sense of adventure?"

Alex grabbed some glasses from inside his room and met the two men at the top of the lighthouse.

The view was beautiful, never failing to take his breath away. Alex had been delighted with the suggestion to hold the bachelor party on the observation platform. In fact, he planned to have his own bachelor send-off up there, if it ever came to be, no matter how remote that possibility looked at the time.

Les was still out of breath by the time Alex joined them at the top, and he was afraid they might have to carry the older man back down after a few drinks.

Mor must have been thinking the same thing. "Are you doing okay, partner?"

"Fine," he said, panting slightly. "Just need to get my wind back," he added. After a few moments, Les said, "Enough of this foolishness. It's time for a toast." He popped the cork off the champagne and poured the bubbling liquid into each of the glasses.

After setting the bottle down, Les lifted his glass and the others joined him. He looked at Mor a second, then said, "To you, Mordecai Pendleton, the best partner, and best friend a man could ask for."

Alex added, "To Mor, the true best man," as the three men clinked their glasses together.

Mor, uncomfortable with the raw sincerity of his friends, said, "Drink up before it goes flat."

Les killed his drink with one pull, then said, "You boys can have the beer, but I'd be proud to keep you company a little while longer. If I'm going to get down those steps on my own, I'd better stop drinking right now. Don't let that stop you two, though."

Alex leaned against the lighthouse, his back against the

solid wall of the structure. He felt grounded whenever he touched it, as if his body became, for one instant, a part of the lighthouse itself.

Alex asked Mor, "Any nerves about tomorrow?"

"I just wish it were already over. You know how I hate a fuss."

Les said, "Listen, nobody's going to be looking at you. This wedding is Emma's time to shine. The best advice I can give you is to take one step back and let her glow."

"Why should I take wedding advice from a grizzled old bachelor like you?" Mor asked, teasing his friend with their usual banter.

Les wasn't having any of it, though, not tonight. "Take it from a man who's spent his life looking for what you've found, my friend. She's a keeper." With a wink to Alex, Les added, "If you hadn't gotten off your duff and asked her to marry you, I might have gone after her myself. She's a big, handsome woman, just the kind I fancy."

Mor said, "Sorry to disappoint you, but you're just going to have to find somebody else. I'm not about to let her go."

Les patted Alex on the shoulder. "Looks like after tomorrow it's just the two of us."

Mor said, "Speak for yourself. Alex has his heart set on Elise."

Les shook his head. "Just remember me when you're both happy and married off, will you?"

Alex said, "After my first-date disaster with her? I don't think you have to worry about me any time soon."

Mor said, "I've got faith in you, buddy."

"Thanks for the vote of confidence. I can tell how sincere you are by the certainty in your voice."

"What? No, it's not that. I just wish . . . never mind."

"Go ahead," Alex said. "What is it?"

Mor said, "What I would have really liked is for Armstrong to have figured out who killed Toby Sturbridge before the wedding. I'm afraid it's going to hang over our heads like an ax tomorrow at the ceremony."

Les said, "Alex and I know you and your bride are innocent, and most of Elkton Falls knows it, too. Don't fret about things you can't change."

Mor smiled gently. "You're just full of advice tonight, aren't you?"

Les said, "Pay no attention to me. It's the alcohol talking. Gentlemen, if you'll excuse me, I'm turning in early tonight. I want to be fresh as a daisy for the festivities tomorrow."

Mor asked, "Do you want me to go down the steps with you?"

Les snapped, "I may be more than twice as old as you are, but I'm a long way from feeble. You two finish up your little party here. I'll be fine."

Both men leaned over the rail until they saw Les down below. He waved up at them, then got into his truck and drove back toward town.

Alex and Mor looked off into the distance, taking in the moonlit land beneath them, enjoying the silence of good company.

"What we really need is a good fog," Alex said. "There's nothing like it from up here."

Mor said, "I'd just as soon the weather stay clear until after the wedding." He gestured down to the canopy set up below for the wedding tomorrow. "I'm still not sure it was such a great idea doing this outdoors. We're probably going to get edges of rain from that hurricane."

Alex said, "Buddy, it was an argument you were bound to lose. Don't worry, I've ordered fair weather until the ceremony, and just to be sure, I didn't wash my truck. That's a sure sign of clear skies."

Mor said, "I appreciate the sacrifice, but you'd better park in back of the inn or Emma will have you out there washing it before the wedding."

Alex grinned. "I've got a feeling tomorrow she's going to be too busy to worry about me." Alex took a breath, then added, "Just between the two of us, are you nervous at all?"

Mor shook his head. "Not one bit. Emma drives me crazy most of the time, but she also makes me happy for no reason at all. When this thing blew up and we were apart, I missed her in a thousand different ways." Realizing how serious his tone had become, Mor added lightly, "Besides, at this point, she's probably the only one who'll have me."

Alex laughed. "If you're waiting for me to disagree with you, I wouldn't hold my breath."

Mor said, "Enough of this. I'm ready to hit the sack. Thanks again for letting me stay out here."

"I'm glad to have you," Alex said.

As they started back down, Alex suddenly realized that they hadn't opened a single beer. Not only that, but there was still half a bottle of champagne left.

It would probably go on record as the mildest bachelor party in the history of Elkton Falls.

19

"**I hope it** doesn't rain," Elise said, staring out the window the next day at the dark clouds on the horizon. It was an hour before the wedding ceremony, and she and Alex were both busy with last-minute preparations.

Alex said, "We could always have it in here, couldn't we?" He gestured around the lobby. "If we move the tables and sofas into a couple of the guest rooms, we could get the folding chairs in here and make an aisle."

Elise studied it a moment, then said, "I don't think everyone will fit."

Emma came in frowning. "It's not going to rain, and we're not moving this wedding inside."

Alex said, "Easy, Emma, we're just trying to come up with a backup plan."

Emma walked to the windows, scowled up at the sky, and declared, "We'll be fine until tonight. It's just the front from the hurricane." She looked at Elise and said, "I need help getting ready. You've got experience with beauty queen makeup. Can you do anything with me?"

Elise laughed softly. "As if you need it. Come on, I

know a few tricks, but if you ask me, we'll just be gilding the lily."

Emma smiled. "I haven't been a lily in years." She frowned at Alex and added, "Shouldn't you be with the groom? Did you steal his car keys and let the air out of his tires like I asked you to?"

"There's not a chance in the world he's going anywhere," Alex said.

"That's what I thought with Toby Sturbridge, but it took him three times to actually make it to the church. I should have seen that as a sign from above."

Alex said, "Emma, Mor Pendleton is no Toby Sturbridge. You're getting a good man, and he's getting a fine woman."

She kissed him lightly on the cheek. "Thanks, Alex. I guess we'll see you soon."

After they were gone, Alex wondered what Mor was up to. He finally found him talking to Grady Hatch outside where the festivities were set to take place. The mayor had graciously agreed to give Emma away before he left on his big trip to see the world, even though the election was still in dispute.

Alex joined them and said, "There you are, Mor. What's going on?"

Grady said, "The board of elections is still going crazy. They aren't anywhere close to declaring a winner. I've heard of horse races before, but this is ridiculous."

"Can't wait to hand over the reins yourself, can you," Alex said.

Mor said, "Have you seen his motor home? It's a real beauty."

Grady said, "I got more for the house than I had any right to expect, so I decided to go all out. As soon as the reception's over, I'm hitting the road, whether you good people have a new mayor or not."

Alex looked up at the clouds. "Are you sure you don't want to wait this storm out? It might be better driving after this front passes through."

Mor said, "It's not going to rain, Alex. Emma's been

glued to the Weather Channel for the last two days. These are just the edges of the big storm south and east of us."

Alex replied, "Yeah, but how are your knees feeling?" Mor had damaged his knees playing football, and they were a pair of the best barometers around town.

He admitted, "They're a little shaky."

Grady slapped him on the back. "That's not the weather, it's just wedding jitters." He looked at his empty glass and said, "If you gentlemen will excuse me, I think it's time for another drink."

Alex said, "You'd better take it easy on those. We don't want you stumbling down the aisle and falling over Emma's train."

"It's soda, Alex," Grady said shortly, then saw the man's grin. "Though I might freshen it up just a bit from the bar. After all, it's a day for celebration."

After he was gone, Alex asked Mor, "Seriously, how are you doing?"

"Hey, I'd be lying if I said I wasn't just a little nervous. Have you seen Emma? How is she holding up?"

"The last time I saw her, she was scowling at the clouds, daring it to rain."

Mor smiled broadly. "That sounds just like her. Alex, I can't tell you how excited I am. I'm a lucky man."

"You are at that. Is there anything you need?"

"Just to get this thing moving so we can get on with our lives. You know I'm not fond of crowds, and I swear, Emma has invited most of Elkton Falls."

Alex nodded. "It won't be long now. Remember, I've got your airline tickets on my dresser. You're flying out of Charlotte tonight, but you'll have plenty of time to get there after the reception. Did Armstrong give you any grief about going?"

Mor said, "He thought about it, but Emma put a knot in his tail about the whole thing. We're just going to be gone a week, it's not like we're never coming back. You know, I never thought about taking a cruise for a honeymoon, but Emma talked me into it."

Alex laughed. "What was it, the women in bikinis or the meals served seven times a day you were opposed to?"

Mor said, "No Bikini Barbies for me, those gals are too skinny. I like Emma, her shape's got flair, you know what I mean?"

"So it's the food," Alex asked with a grin.

"Who could say no to a midnight buffet? I'm planning to gain at least ten pounds." For the hundredth time, Mor looked at his watch. "I can't believe the wedding's still an hour away."

"I've got an idea. Why don't we go up to your room? I've got a backgammon board set up. It might take your mind off the clock."

Mor said, "I'll give it a shot, but I'm not making any promises about what kind of game I'll be able to play."

Mor normally won the lion's share of the games they played, but this time Alex won every match.

He thought it was fair to say his best friend was more than a little distracted by the events to come.

The crowd was in place, all of Elkton Falls dressed in their finery awaiting the start of the ceremony. Alex and Mor took their spots up front, and Alex nodded to Father Gray, the local Episcopal priest. He and the padre had been friends since grade school, but Alex still couldn't get used to seeing him dressed in his priestly robes.

Gray said softly, "Are you boys ready?"

Alex said, "I'm fine, but Mor keeps trying to make a run for it."

Gray smiled and said, "If you do, I might just marry the gal myself."

Mor shook his head. "You'd have to go through me, priest or no priest."

Gray said, "That's the spirit."

Alex heard Irma Bean suddenly increase the volume of her organ, and his gaze went to the back of the canopy.

Elise was there, holding a bouquet of flowers, wearing an emerald dress that highlighted her green eyes. Her hair was pulled back with wisps trailing down, and she was the most breathtaking vision he'd ever seen in his life. Sometimes it was easy to forget how beautiful she really was as the two of them worked side by side cleaning rooms or washing clothes. But she'd outdone herself this time, and Alex felt his knees grow weak again at the sight of her.

As she marched toward him, Alex couldn't hide his feelings from her, and he was rewarded with her warmest smile.

As she approached, Alex whispered to her, "You look stunning."

"So do you," she said as she took her position across from him. Alex was in his only suit, since Mor had drawn the line against either one of them wearing tuxedoes.

Mor said, "Hey, we're here for me, remember?"

Alex tore his gaze off Elise and looked back up the aisle.

Emma marched in on Grady's arm, and she was truly lovely. Mor was right. Emma was elegant, a large-scale woman full of grace and beauty, and there wasn't a single man in the audience that didn't envy Mor just a little.

Alex saw a tear creep down Emma's cheek as she approached them, and he shifted his gaze to Mor.

The big man had a tear of his own that burrowed deep into his smile.

As Grady gave Emma's arm to Mor, Alex knew that these two truly belonged together.

"I can't believe it didn't rain," Elise said as she and Alex danced during the reception after the vows had been exchanged.

"It was afraid to," Alex admitted, reveling in holding Elise in his arms. "You're a wonderful dancer," he said.

"I can't help myself. I took ballet for ten years when I was growing up, and the rest just seemed to follow."

"Gosh, and I didn't even go to Arthur Murray. The only dance class I took was in college."

"You majored in business, didn't you?" she asked.

"I did, but senior year I needed one elective, so I signed up for ballroom dance."

She laughed. "That's not what I think of as a breeze class."

He said, "Think about it. There were twenty-six students in the class, and only two of us were guys."

He accented his words by twirling her, a move Elise picked up solely from his hand pressure. They danced together as if they'd been doing it for years.

"I'm having a wonderful time," he admitted.

"I am too, Alex. They belong together, don't they," she said as she looked at Emma and Mor.

Alex saw the new bride and groom dancing to their own music in the center of the temporary stage. He said, "It's a match. From what Mor told me, the sheriff's not too happy about them leaving town for six days for their honeymoon, but Emma probably threatened to stick him with the bill for their cruise if they couldn't go, so he backed right down. It's not like they aren't coming straight back, and Armstrong knows it."

Elise said hesitantly, "Alex, I've been meaning to talk to you about something."

"I'm right here," he said as he held her close.

The music died, and they found themselves rocking to a beat that was only between the two of them.

The lead singer said, "Now it's time for the toasts. May we have the best man and maid of honor up on stage?"

Alex said, "What was it you wanted to talk about?"

"It can wait," she said as she took his hand. "It's time for the toasts."

The waiters were handing out champagne as they walked forward, and Alex snagged a pair of glasses for them before they walked up the steps.

On stage, Elise offered to go first, knowing Alex's dread of public speaking. She took the microphone and said, "When two people find each other in this world, it is truly a cause to celebrate. Mor and Emma, I wish you the greatest happiness as you start your lives together, and may your love grow stronger from this day forward. To Mor and Emma."

The crowd lifted their glasses and repeated the last line. Alex felt his heart tighten in his chest, knowing it was his turn now.

Elise patted his hand softly, then whispered, "You'll be fine."

Emboldened by her touch, Alex said, "I've known Mor all my life, and it feels like I've known Emma that long, too. All I've got to say is, you two deserve each other."

That got a laugh from the crowd, one Alex hadn't intended.

"No, what I meant to say was, you belong together. That's it." Blast it all, he'd made a mess of his toast. "To Mor and Emma," he said, and again the crowd raised their glasses to the newlyweds.

Elise joined him and said, "Alex Winston, that was a bold move. I never would have imagined you'd go for humor."

"I didn't mean to," he admitted as they walked offstage.

Elise tried to hide her smile, but couldn't. "You were wonderful."

And then she kissed him.

There was nothing odd or awkward about it. It was almost as if the two of them melted together for a moment, lost in each other's arms.

Alex was jarred out of it by the mayor's hand on his shoulder. "Hey, I thought the tradition was to kiss the bride, but if it's the maid of honor now, I'm next in line."

At that moment, Alex could have easily killed Grady Hatch on the spot with his bare hands.

Elise looked startled by their kiss. "I've got to go help Emma get ready for their getaway."

"Hang on a second, Elise," Alex said, wanting to hold on to the moment.

"Later, Alex. There'll be time later."

As she disappeared into the crowd of dancers, Grady said, "Something tells me my timing was rotten there."

Alex said, "Don't worry about it."

"No, I'm sorry. Alex, I must have had too much to drink. I'm not usually this dense. Tell you what, I'm going over to my motor home and taking a nap before I hit the road. I'm not in any condition to drive."

"You can stay at the inn. We're just about empty right now."

Grady said, "Thanks, but that's why I got my new wheels. I've got my bed with me wherever I go now."

As Grady teetered off to his new abode, Alex felt a meaty hand on his shoulder. Mor said, "Did I just see what I thought I did?"

Alex felt his face flush. "I don't know, what did you see?"

"Don't mess with me, Alex. Did you just kiss Elise?"

He shrugged. "You know how weddings affect people."

"That wasn't just because of the wedding, my friend. I guess you finally found a way to break the ice with her."

Alex said, "I wouldn't be so sure. Did you see how fast she just ran away? When Grady Hatch interrupted us, I thought she was going to run back into the inn."

"Talk to her, Alex. Don't let her get away again."

Alex said, "Mor, I never had her to begin with." He slapped his friend on the back. "Don't you have anything better to do than worry about me? When are you'all getting out of here?"

"Trying to get rid of us already?" Mor asked with a grin. "As soon as Emma tosses her bouquet, we're on our way. I'd better go see what's keeping her."

Five minutes later they were ready to go, with everyone milling around waiting for them. Emma tossed the bouquet over her shoulder, and Alex was certain it was no accident that it landed squarely in Elise's arms.

She looked as if she'd caught a live snake, but Elise somehow managed to be gracious about it until the spotlight of attention left her.

After the newlyweds drove away in Emma's decorated car, the reception started breaking up. There were more than a few glances at the oncoming clouds, and the planners looked anxious to break camp and get everything packed up.

It appeared they were in for one whale of a storm.

Alex found Elise inside, staring at the bouquet in her hands.

"Nice catch," he said as he loosened his tie.

"Alex, we've got to talk about what happened."

He said, "Hey, it's just an old wives' tale. Nobody expects you to get married next."

She said, "That's not what I mean. We have to talk about that kiss."

Alex looked steadily at her. "Why? Why can't we just enjoy it?"

"Alex, I was swept up in the emotion of the moment. It was a mistake."

"How can you say that?" Alex asked, fighting to keep his voice in control. "It didn't feel like a mistake to me."

"I'm not ready," she said softly. "I was engaged not that long ago."

"Elise, I'm not pushing you. We can take our time, but you can't deny there were sparks between us."

She said gently, "It was most likely the champagne."

He held her gaze. "I don't believe that for one second, and I don't think you do either. It was us."

"Oh, Alex," was all she said before she rushed to her room.

So she'd thought their shared kiss was a mistake. Normally Alex would have been shattered by the revelation, by the rejection.

But this time it was different.

No matter how much she protested, Alex knew that Elise had been as moved by the kiss as he'd been.

And hope sparked in his heart again.

20

"We're looking for Grady Hatch. Has he been out here?" Conner Shook asked as he burst into the inn.

Alex was stunned to see Tracy following just behind her ex-husband.

He said, "He's sleeping one off in his camper. What's the emergency?"

Tracy said, "Let me handle this, Conner. Alex, we need him to step in and take over this election. The board is making a real mess of it."

Conner added, "If Shantara would keep her mouth shut and let them finish one count without butting in, we'd have been done last night."

"She's looking out for my best interests, Conner. I've got the same complaint with Gladys Rhine."

"Hey, she's making sure you don't slip in the back door of the mayor's office," Conner protested.

Alex said, "Listen, I don't need to hear this. Go talk to Grady."

They both left, heading out for the motor home where the mayor was about to get a rude awakening.

One minute after they left, the rain started abruptly,

pounding down in sudden fierce waves of monstrous drops. There was no drizzle beforehand, no warning that such violence was imminent. At least it had waited until all the guests were gone, Alex mused, as he watched the fierce attack of the deluge.

Elise came downstairs, back in blue jeans and a polo shirt, her hair pulled into its traditional ponytail. She still looked lovely to him.

"Wow, that's an incredible storm," she said as she looked out the window. "You can barely see the lighthouse from here."

It was true. Alex couldn't remember seeing such a hard rain in all his years at Hatteras West.

Elise said, "I'm going to turn on the radio and see if there's anything on the news about it."

As she switched on the radio that was sitting on an end table, they heard, ". . . shelter. To repeat, Hurricane Zelda is heading straight for Elkton Falls. Those without basements are advised to head to the high school bomb shelter. Folks, this one's going to be a direct hit. Charlotte got skirted, but Hickory was slammed full on. Now she's coming our way, fast and mean. To repeat, Hurricane Zelda . . ." Elise turned the volume down.

"Mor and Emma are on the road, and they're driving right into a hurricane."

Alex said, "Chances are they're already in Charlotte. I've never been happier that the inn is empty. If this thing had hit yesterday or tomorrow, we'd have real problems on our hands."

Elise said, "Alex, you don't have a basement here. Should we head over to the high school?"

Alex shook his head. "We're safer in the lighthouse, Elise. Think about it. Both Hatteras lighthouses, east and west, were designed to withstand this kind of punishing weather. If you'd feel better going to the high school, I guess I could go with you," he added.

"No, you're right. I'd feel safer at the lighthouse with you. Alex, we should get over there right now with some supplies."

"That might not be such a bad idea." They worked together again as a team, gathering plastic bins with flashlights, food, and blankets, drawing water for later and battening down the inn as much as they could. He was glad he'd insisted on working storm shutters when they'd rebuilt the Dual Keepers' Quarters. He felt a lot more secure being able to cover the windows. Alex finished pulling the chairs in from the porch and was soaked to the bone by the time he got everything inside. Grady, Conner, and Tracy were already there waiting for him.

Alex took the towel Elise offered and he started drying his hair. "We're going to ride this out in the lighthouse," he told them. "You're welcome to join us."

Conner said, "Do we have any choice? It's getting dangerous out there."

Alex said, "Just let me change, then we'll head over."

Conner said, "Come when you're ready, but I'm going right now." He picked up a bin and headed for the front door.

Grady grabbed one too, then said, "Come on, Tracy, they can manage here."

Tracy followed, and by the time Alex got back downstairs, Elise was waiting for him with the last two bins of supplies. "It's going to be a little crowded in the base with all this stuff."

"Hey, don't forget, we've got the steps to use as seats and shelves. Don't worry, Elise, we're going to be fine."

"I'll feel better once we get over there and get the front doors bolted shut," she admitted.

"Let's go, then," Alex said as he grabbed the heavier bin. The rain was now mixed with hail, and it stung as it pounded into them. Alex stopped to secure the inn's doors, then ran after Elise in the muck and mud. The rain had quickly saturated the ground and had left a quagmire behind.

Once they were with the others inside the base of the lighthouse, Alex bolted the main doors. Very little light came in from the window above their heads, and Alex flipped on one of his powerful flashlights. The white walls reflected the beam, and the interior seemed almost cheerful compared to the howling winds outside. Alex leaned against the circular rail at the base and said, "Looks like we're in this for the long haul. Did anybody hear when the storm shifted so far inland?"

Conner said, "We were too wrapped up in this recount to pay much attention. I think it happened pretty fast."

Grady added, "I should have hit the road four hours ago." He held a hand to his head and said, "What a splitting headache. I think I've just gone on the wagon."

Elise turned on the portable radio and had to raise the volume so they could hear over the roar of the storm outside.

". . . edges have just touched town. Hunker down, folks, the electricity went off ten minutes ago, and we're running off the generator. Stay where you are! If you can't get to a basement, a doorway's good, even a cast-iron tub if you've got one. The eye's due to pass over us in about twenty minutes, but don't go outside because it looks calm. When the back side hits, it's going to have a real punch to it."

They listened for a while as news of devastation farther south trickled in. Charlotte was miraculously bypassed, but a few towns nearby weren't nearly so lucky, getting ravaged by the storm. Hickory had been particularly hard hit, with trees and power lines down all over the city.

"It sounds like a train's out there," Tracy said, the awe for the power of the storm thick in her voice.

"Look at that," Conner said, pointing to the window above them. "The rain's actually falling up. It's like being in a giant car wash."

"I don't need to be here," Grady said.

"Well, we're all stuck for now," Elise said. "So we might as well make the best of it."

Alex said to Grady, "I thought you'd be more interested in your constituents than just wanting to take off."

Grady said, "Of course I am, but it's going to be up to one of these two to rebuild what's ruined. I've served my time here."

Tracy said, "I wonder if the covered bridge is going to

survive this. It would be a shame to lose it after you'all worked so hard to raise money for its restoration."

Grady shrugged. "We didn't raise all that much, just a few bucks, really. I'd hate to see it go, too," he added as he looked down at his shoes.

Without thinking, Alex said, "That's not true at all. I know for a fact there have been several hefty donations to the project."

Grady said, "Alex, aren't you too old to believe in rumors and idle gossip? I've got a feeling a lot of folks are bragging about giving to the fund without cracking their checkbooks."

Conner jumped in. "Oxford told me there was over twenty thousand in the kitty, and that was a good month ago. Is that what you call a few bucks?"

"He was always prone to exaggeration, just like most politicians are," Grady said. "Is the storm letting up? It's not raining nearly as hard as it was."

The mayor started for the handle when Alex stepped in front of him. Everything was starting to come together in his mind, and he didn't want anyone leaving until he tested his theory. Fighting to be heard over the storm, Alex asked, "Is that why you killed Oxford, for the money?"

Grady snapped, "What are you talking about, Alex? Have you lost your mind?"

Alex said, "It just makes sense, doesn't it?" He turned to Conner. "Did you know about it too, or was he just using you?"

Conner sputtered, "Alex, you're certifiably insane."

Alex shook his head. "I don't think so. It all makes sense. Oxford found out Grady was stealing from the bridge fund. It was kind of poetic justice when he confronted you there about your theft. So you killed him."

The warm, friendly mayor they all knew was suddenly replaced by a caged animal ready to strike out.

Grady pulled a gun from his jacket and said, "You had to push it, didn't you, Alex? Well, knowing what happened isn't going to do you a bit of good now."

•　•　•

Tracy said in a stunned voice, "Then it's true?"

Grady waved her over to the rest of the group, away from the door. "Don't look so shocked. All my life I've been serving the people of Elkton Falls. It was about time they started serving me."

Conner said, "Shut up, Hatch."

"You think I'm going down without taking you with me? You knew all about my dipping into the fund."

Conner said, "You lying dog. I didn't know you'd killed Oxford or that troublemaker out in the parking lot, either."

Alex said, "You killed Toby Sturbridge?"

"The fool brought it on himself. Oxford and I thought the parking lot would be the safest place to talk with everybody at the rededication. Oxford demanded I return the money, the do-gooder. Sturbridge must have heard the threats. After Oxford left, I was shaken up pretty good, so I leaned against Mor's truck for a cigarette to settle my nerves. This thug came up and threatened me if I didn't cut him in on what I'd stolen. He grabbed me, I panicked so I pushed him. Okay, maybe it was a little too hard, but I swear, I didn't mean to kill him. I stuck him in the nearest truck and got back up onstage."

"I thought you looked like you had the jitters that day," Alex admitted. "I just couldn't figure out why."

Tracy said, "What did Conner know, Grady? Tell us that much."

"I told you to shut up," Conner said as he started to lunge for Grady's gun.

The mayor held it up, his finger white on the trigger. "Don't make me shoot you, Conner. I'm too favorable toward the idea as it is."

Conner backed off, and Grady finished, "He knew something was going on, but he didn't know quite what the handle was. I couldn't afford any attention, so I promised to help him get elected if he'd stay out of things until after the election. I planned to be long gone by the time he blew the lid off it."

"You can't prove I knew anything about this mess," Conner shouted.

"I don't have to," Grady said. "I'm not a cop."

Alex said, "So what are you going to do now, Grady. You can't kill all of us."

"I'm not some kind of cold-blooded killer, Alex. Sturbridge was a fluke, and Oxford was threatening me. Where I'm going, nobody will ever be able to find me."

"How are you going to get anywhere?" Elise asked. "There's a hurricane out there."

Grady smiled. "It's the perfect cover. Everybody's going to be too busy digging out from under the debris to come after me."

The mayor threw the doors open and looked outside at the eerie calm. Alex could see that a few trees had come down around the property, but remarkably, the inn itself didn't appear to have suffered much damage. There was a shimmering green pall to the light, and a hushed stillness that defied description. It was, to Alex, almost as if he'd gone suddenly deaf, the quiet was so complete.

Conner said, "You'll never make your getaway in a motor home, Grady, not during this storm. Don't be a fool."

"The only fool thing I've done is hang around here too long, and I'm about to correct that right now."

Grady was gone before they could stop him, and Alex fought the urge to go after him.

Elise must have read his mind. "Don't even think about going out there, Alex. It's too dangerous."

"I know, but it's hard just letting him go." Alex knew that the other side of the storm would be there soon enough, and the last place on Earth he wanted to be was out in it, but it still bothered him.

"He's not worth it," Elise said as she bolted the doors.

Alex knew she was right. Let Grady Hatch take his chances with Zelda.

Sooner or later, the police would catch up with him.

There was no doubt in Alex's mind about that.

21

"**What brings you** to Hatteras West?" Alex asked as Elkton Falls' brand-new mayor arrived at the inn a few days later.

"Just checking up on my constituents," Tracy said. "I still can't believe they haven't found Grady yet."

Alex finished sweeping the porch steps and said, "Hey, he's only been gone forty-eight hours. How far could he get on foot?"

The remnants of Grady's motor home still remained under one of the trees Alex had lost in the storm. He would have loved to see the mayor's face when he realized that his getaway car wasn't going anywhere.

"The man's craftier than any of us gave him credit for," Tracy said. "I don't trust him."

"Speaking of trust, what's your ex-husband have to say about all this?"

Tracy smiled. "Oh, he's denied any connection with the mayor, and the sheriff says we don't have enough solid evidence to arrest him, no matter how hard I push it. I do have some good news on that front, though. It seems Conner has decided to relocate. Elkton Falls is suddenly too small for him."

"Where's he going?" Alex asked.

"Out West is all I heard. They're welcome to him. He'll never admit it, but I know now that mannequin was his work."

Alex said, "I still can't believe Grady wiped out the bridge fund and tried to run away with all that money we raised. I thought he really believed in the restoration. I'm going to head over there later and see if anything happened to the bridge during the storm. Have you heard anything about our electricity?"

"Duke Power said we'll have most of our service back in a day or two. What are you doing about your guests?"

"Nobody showed up," Alex admitted. "Being directly in the path of a hurricane doesn't exactly inspire folks to vacation here." He added, "Don't worry about us, though, we'll manage to squeak by somehow."

"You always do, don't you?"

Elise came outside and said, "Hey, Ms. Mayor."

Tracy laughed. "That's going to take some getting used to, hearing that."

"I think you'll manage," Alex said.

"Oh yes," Tracy admitted. "Well, I just wanted to touch base with you all. Alex, if you need anything out here, just let me know. I owe you one."

Alex grinned. "I'll remind you of that when I ask you to push the Town Council about letting me light my lens more than once a year."

Tracy nodded. "You've got yourself a deal. Let me dig out of all this hurricane mess and we'll talk about it then."

"Sounds good to me."

After Tracy was gone, Elise said, "I just heard from Emma."

They'd been trying to track the newlyweds down since the storm, without any success.

"Did they make it all right?" Alex asked.

"So far they've spent their honeymoon at Charlotte-

Douglas Airport. There's nothing to worry about, though, they should be leaving for their cruise today."

"Hasn't the ship already left port?" Alex asked.

"Yes, but they're meeting it at the first stop. Emma was understandably relieved to hear that Grady confessed to killing Toby in front of witnesses."

Alex said, "Do you think she still thought Mor might have had something to do with it?"

Elise shrugged. "Well, she married him, didn't she?"

"That doesn't answer my question."

"Does it really matter, Alex? They're together. Ultimately, that's all that counts."

Alex leaned his broom against the wall and said, "We need to have another talk, Elise. I'm not happy with the way we left things."

"There's nothing to talk about," Elise said.

"You might not think so, but I surely do."

Sheriff Armstrong drove up Point Road in his cruiser, and Elise said, "Not now, Alex. Not with the sheriff coming."

"He can wait."

Elise shook her head, touched Alex's cheek lightly, then said, "So can this discussion."

Armstrong got out of his cruiser and said, "The storm wasn't too bad out here, was it?"

"I don't even have to call Smiley O'Reilly," Alex admitted. "I'll bet he's been hopping the last few days."

Armstrong nodded. "I don't think the man's had a wink of sleep since the storm hit. Some folks got slammed pretty hard, and some it barely touched." Shifting his feet, the sheriff added, "Just thought you might want to know, seeing how you were involved in all this. They just found Grady Hatch."

"Where was he, heading for the border?"

Armstrong shook his head. "He never made it that far. From the look of things, he tried to head out on foot when he saw his camper all bashed in. The storm must have picked him up and thrown him like an old rag doll. I won't even make you guess where his body finally ended up.

He's not twenty feet from the spot where he killed Oxford Hitchcock."

"I never would have believed him capable of murder," Alex admitted.

"Funny thing, you never know what's going to set a body off like that. Well, I'd better get back into town. I just wanted to let you know."

"Thanks, Sheriff," Alex said.

After he was gone, Alex stayed outside, staring up at the lighthouse. He'd survived his second hurricane inside its safe walls, the first one since he'd been born on that Halloween night years and years ago. It was there for him always, a haven of safety when the world around him was going insane.

Alex looked back inside through the window of the Main Keeper's Quarters and saw Elise working at the registration desk.

No matter how hard she tried, there was no way Elise could deny the power of that kiss they'd shared.

He'd just have to find a way to convince her that it had been right and good, and not a mistake.

It could be tough going, given Elise's vulnerability and her fear about ruining their friendship.

But he'd do his best to show her that they belonged together as more than just friends.

It was definitely a task worth taking on.

About the Author

Tim Myers lives with his family near the Blue Ridge Mountains he loves and writes about. He is the award-winning author of the Agatha-nominated Lighthouse Inn mystery series as well as more than seventy short stories.

Coming February 2004, *At Wick's End* is the first in Tim's new Candlemaking mystery series, also from Berkley Prime Crime.

Tim has been a stay-at-home dad for the last twelve years, finding time for murder and mayhem whenever he can.

To learn more, visit his website at **www.timmyers.net** or contact him at **timothylmyers@hotmail.com**.